She didn't look up when the door opened—not until she heard his voice.

Standing up quickly, she looked into the warm blue eyes of the man she had traveled all this way to see. She tried to speak his name, but her mouth was too dry to make a sound.

"Emily," Jonathan said quietly, looking into her eyes.

In that moment, without a word or a touch, Emily sensed her life was bound to this man's.

"Your biscuits are burning," Phineas said.

"Oh!" Emily knelt down on the hearth to pull the pan back from the reflected heat.

"We brought back some of the first syrup. Over biscuits it will be the sweetest treat you ever tasted," Sally declared. "Are those made with wheat flour? I haven't tasted wheat flour in years." She hugged Emily. "You're a dear to make them for us."

"Here's the syrup," Jonathan said, as he extended a jug toward Emily.

All else in the room faded as Emily searched his face. She felt as if they were alone in their own world. He returned her steady gaze until Sally took the jug from his hand, breaking the breathtaking moment.

MARILOU H. FLINKMAN can't stay out of prison. She is highly active in prison ministry in her home state of Washington where she encourages prisoners to make right choices in the future and give past mistakes to the forgiving Father in Heaven. Marilou also teaches beginning writing to college students while she adds to her own list of well over 100 published short stories and articles. Her best friend happens to be her husband, and they have six living children and nine grandchildren scattered throughout the Northwest. Her hobbies include reading about 100 books a year, traveling, and fishing.

HEARTSONG PRESENTS

Books by Marilou H. Flinkman
HP258—The Alaskan Way
HP442—Vision of Hope

Sweet Spring

Marilou H. Flinkman

Heartsong Presents

Entreat me not to leave thee,
or to return from following after thee:
for whither thou goest, I will go;
and where thou lodgest, I will lodge:
thy people shall be my people, and thy God my God.
Ruth 1:16

A note from the author:
I love to hear from my readers! You may correspond with me
by writing: **Marilou H. Flinkman**
                         Author Relations
                         PO Box 719
                         Uhrichsville, OH 44683

ISBN 1-58660-385-X

SWEET SPRING

All Scripture quotations are taken from the King James Version of the Bible.

Cover illustration by Gary Maria.

PRINTED IN THE U.S.A.

one

The crisp air of February caused Emily Goodman to pull her shawl closer around her shoulders. Walking next to her mother, she saw the white steeple of the Ashford, Connecticut, church framed against the deep blue winter sky.

"Can't you keep your hair controlled?" Mother asked crossly as the two approached the church.

Emily tried to tuck several straying brown tendrils back under her bonnet. She glanced at her mother's hair, pulled back into such a tight bun that her forehead looked tortured.

Just then Mother stopped to speak to Mrs. Gardner, who'd just joined them on the path to the church. Emily noticed that her mother's smile did not reach her eyes and marveled at how, at five feet nothing, Mother could still look down her nose at most people around her.

Emily searched for her sister in the crowd gathering at the church.

"May I sit with Elizabeth?" she quietly asked.

"Can you sit up straight and not whisper?"

"Yes, Mother." Emily tried not to show how much she chafed at being treated like a wayward child.

Her father joined them and took her mother's arm. "I've tethered the horse and buggy. Let's go in and find a seat." His jovial, good nature warmed Emily's heart. He towered over the women, and his snow-white hair and ruddy complexion stood out in the crowd entering the building.

"Emily wants to sit with Elizabeth," Mother said with disapproval in her voice.

Father put an arm around Emily's shoulder and kissed her cheek. "Go along with you. It is nice to see my girls worship together." He guided Mother down the isle before she could say more.

Gratefully, Emily slipped into the space next to Elizabeth and David.

"How did you manage to escape?" Beth whispered.

"Father saved me. Oh, Beth, Mother keeps getting worse and worse since you got married. I can't bear to think of what it will be like when you and David move to the New York frontier."

The minister stood at the front of the church with an open Bible. The young women listened with great interest as he read from the Scriptures, explaining what each passage meant.

Fantasies soon stole Emily's mind away from the minister's message. She glanced covertly about the sanctuary for David's brother. She and Jonathan were both seventeen, but he never seemed to notice she existed. *Now he's moving away,* she lamented inwardly.

She thought about the plans of David and Jonathan's father to move to central New York State where land was available. *How will I ever live without Beth to run to?* she asked herself. *And now I'll never get to know Jonathan better.*

The sun shining through the windows reminded Emily that the snow would soon melt, and the Miller family would be off to find a new home.

"Would you like to come home with us for dinner?" Beth asked.

Startled, Emily realized the service had ended, and she couldn't remember a bit of the sermon. She tried to look for her parents, but standing barely an inch taller than her mother, she couldn't see over the people gathered at the door to greet the minister.

"They are over there." David pointed toward the right side of the church.

"Thanks, David. If I can ask when Father is there, he'll make Mother let me go home with you."

"Emily, you make our mother sound like a witch," Beth scolded quietly.

"Elizabeth!" Emily said in shock.

Beth laughed. "They haven't burned a witch around here in over a hundred years. She is safe."

"Oh, she is talking to Henry Richards. I'd better get to them quickly before she invites him for dinner. He's repulsive, and Mother is determined to make me marry him." Emily hurried to her father's side.

"Look who's here," Mother cooed, taking hold of the smug-looking man. Henry's stomach stretched his vest buttons to the popping point. His smile appeared as greasy as his slicked down hair. *He has skinny eyes,* Emily thought with an inward shudder, looking at the beady eyes glittering at her out from crinkles of fat.

Emily smiled weakly and nodded at Henry as she touched her father's arm. "Elizabeth and David have invited me to dinner. You don't mind if I go, do you?"

Her father hugged her. "Better visit with her while you can. She and David will be moving as soon as the weather breaks."

Mother frowned. "I suppose that George Miller will be there. All he ever talks about is how he fought in the Revolution. The war ended over twenty-five years ago," she said, sniffing in disapproval.

"Now, Maggie. Mr. Miller is a good man. He took good care of his wife Isobel until she died, then he raised two fine boys by himself."

Mother glowered at Father but did not speak.

Emily reached up to give her father a kiss on the cheek and saw her mother's look of displeasure.

"Good-bye, Mother," Emily muttered, hurrying away.

❧

"Can you stand another round of my father's war stories?" David asked Emily as the three young people walked home from church.

Emily laughed. "Anything is better than watching Henry Richards stuff his face. He is so fat he jiggles when he walks."

"He is a bit overweight." David grinned. "Maybe if he would work a little more at the mercantile he would lose some. He's going to have to help his father more when we move west."

"Mr. Richards will certainly miss you as a clerk," Beth told her husband, looking up at his blue eyes and sandy blond hair.

Emily's heart contracted. She saw the adoration her sister and David shared and wondered if she would ever have love like that. *Not if you stay around here and have to marry that smug Henry Richards.*

They entered the small house David and Beth rented. Emily headed for the kitchen to stoke the woodstove and put the kettle on for tea. Soon Beth joined her and began preparations for the noon meal, while Emily took hot tea to Mr. Miller and his two sons.

Emily handed Jonathan a cup, her hand trembling, but his vivid blue eyes scarcely seemed to see her. She noticed that his hair, the same sandy blond color as his brother's, was held neatly at the nape of his neck with a black band. He was listening to his father talk about the land he had seen near Lake Ontario when he had fought in the Revolutionary War.

"Father, the war has been over for years. How do you know the land is the same as you remember?" David asked.

Mr. Miller walked around the room with his cup in his hand. "I've kept in contact with people who have been there." He took a sip of the tea. "You know I came back here from the war to marry your mother. I wanted to go then, but her health was never good." He looked sadly at his sons. "Do you even remember her?"

"Only a little. I couldn't have been more than five or six when she died," David answered.

"Why did you keep fishing after she died? Why didn't you

go west then?" Jonathan asked.

Mr. Miller smiled. "I had you boys to raise. I couldn't do that and build a home in the wilderness at the same time."

"I don't care for fishing," Jonathan declared. "I can't wait to have land and grow apples."

Both David and his father laughed. "You and those apples. What makes you think they'll grow near the lake?"

"I got a book about it. It sounds like the climate there is perfect to start an orchard. I have ordered seedlings to take out with us."

"You're going to carry apple trees in your saddlebags?" David asked in wonder.

"Why not?" Jonathan drew himself to his full height. He stood a bit taller than his brother.

Emily, waiting to serve more tea, listened to every word. "I think apples will be very nice," she said quietly.

Jonathan turned to look at her. She felt her cheeks burn at his full attention. "I am glad someone agrees with me." He held his cup up for her to refill with tea.

Emily poured more into his cup, all the while gazing into his eyes, until he smiled and looked down at the cup. She gasped when she realized she had filled it to the brim. If the pot hadn't emptied just then, she would have poured tea onto the floor. Feeling her face grow hot, she fled to the kitchen in embarrassment.

"Is David's father winning the war again?" Beth asked with a grin, when Emily hurried through the door.

"They are talking about the land you're going to. Oh, Beth are you sure you can stand the frontier?"

" 'Whither thou goest,' " Beth replied, "and my husband is going to settle in Scriba's Patent, where his father plans to buy land."

Emily wrapped Beth in a hug. "How I wish I could go too."

"We just have to trust the Lord to work out the details." Beth turned to stir a bubbling pot on the stove.

"You think there is a way?" Emily stood back to watch her sister. "Do you think I can go too?" she asked hopefully.

"All things are possible in God," Beth said quietly, then went about serving the fish her father-in-law had caught the day before.

"Very good dinner," Mr. Miller complimented his son's wife as he pushed himself back from the table.

"Have you heard from the land agent about buying lots?" David asked his father.

"I received a message this week. It seems this Mr. Scriba owns the Dutch patent on a large grant of land around Lake Ontario in the northern part of New York. He owns a grist-mill in Rotterdam, so he doesn't want all the land. He'll sell forty-acre lots for twenty dollars down. As long as we keep up the yearly interest, we can develop the land. I plan to put money down on a lot for each of you."

"But how will we be able to keep up the interest payments?" Jonathan asked. "My apples won't become a cash crop for years."

"Apples?" Beth asked.

"Jonathan is taking seedlings in his saddlebags. Has a dream of a vast orchard someday." George smiled with pride when he looked at his younger son.

"But where will we get money to pay the interest?" Jonathan asked again.

"We sell ashes!"

The four young people looked at Mr. Miller as though he had lost his wits.

"Ashes?" Beth whispered.

The boys' father guffawed at their expressions. "I've been talking to people who have come back from the Four Corners and Colosse area. In a good year, we can sell ashes for nine cents a barrel to the Potash Company. They use it for making soap and glass." He looked around at the young people watching him. "We have a lot of trees to cut down and burn to clear for planting. We can use some of the ashes as fertilizer for our fields, but we'll have much more than we need."

"I guess if I am going to have land for an orchard, I have to cut down the trees already there," Jonathan admitted.

"Now you are beginning to understand," Mr. Miller said, nodding.

The men continued to make plans for the move, while Emily and Beth cleared the table and washed the dishes.

"You're very quiet, Beth. Are you all right?"

Beth nodded her head. "I am a little tired is all." She looked out the window where the sun was setting.

"You had better start home. Mother will never let you come again if you don't return before dark."

"Thank you for inviting me. I am ashamed to admit it, but I like to get away from Mother. I cannot do anything to please her anymore," Emily groaned as she hugged her sister.

Beth giggled. "You could marry Henry Richards."

Emily shuddered. "He looks like a toad."

They hugged again. "Keep praying, Emmy. God will take care of us."

two

The next afternoon, while her mother went visiting, Emily sat plying her needle to piecing a quilt top and dreaming of Jonathan. She jumped up in pleasure when her sister came through the door.

"Is Mother here?"

Emily shook her head. "She's having tea at Mrs. Gardner's."

"Good—I wanted to talk to you," Beth said, crossing to the mantel.

Emily put her sewing by the side of her chair as she sat down. "What is it Beth? You look so sad."

Beth stood by the low fire with her back to her sister and didn't answer.

"Are you having second thoughts about going to New York?" Emily asked in concern.

"Something like that." Beth poked at the embers in the fireplace.

"Let me make us some tea. Why don't you come to the kitchen? We can visit while we wait for the water to boil."

Beth sat at the table watching Emily put tea leaves in the pot. "I am going to miss this."

Emily looked up at her sister after putting the lid on the tea canister. "I don't know how I'll manage without you. It has been hard enough these last months since your marriage, not having you in the house all the time."

"Don't you like having a room all to yourself?" Beth smiled.

"Sure," Emily said. "I'm glad to see you smile, Beth. But why did you look so glum when you came in? Are you afraid to move?"

Beth took a spoon from the holder in the middle of the

table and turned it about in her hand. "I want to go—but not for awhile," she said quietly.

Emily poured boiling water over the tea leaves and reached for the cups. "I don't understand. If you're afraid now, what makes you think it will be better later?"

Beth waited for Emily to sit down. Then she took her sister's hands. "I'm going to have a baby."

"Oh! How wonderful!" Emily put her hand over her mouth. "But what are you going to do?"

"I don't know."

"Have you talked to David?"

Beth shook her head. "I'm afraid he'll be so disappointed."

"Disappointed! He is going to be delighted!"

"But now I don't want to go west until after the baby is born. It's one thing to start over in the wilderness, but not when I'm having my first baby," Beth cried.

Emily started to giggle.

"What is so funny?"

"Mother. Can you picture our mother as a grandma?"

Beth joined Emily's infectious laughter. "She doesn't like to admit her age. This will be quite a change for her."

"Father will bust his buttons," Emily predicted.

"All the more reason I should have the baby here where they can see him before I move west."

"You have already decided it's a boy?"

Beth smiled and picked up her teacup. "I know that would please David." She put the cup back down without taking a sip. "I'll have to do something to make up for his not going out with his father and brother."

"You better talk to him right away. Plans will have to be changed."

"You're right, as usual." Beth stood up. "I'll go fix him a good supper and tell him tonight." She hugged her sister. "It always helps to talk to you. I'm older and should be your helper—not the other way around."

Emily hugged her sister back. "We are here for each other." She didn't add that she would try to talk her parents into letting her go with Beth and David when they moved. *Beth will need my help with the baby.*

❧

Emily prevailed upon her mother to invite David and Beth for Sunday dinner. But no amount of coaxing could get her to include David's father and brother.

At supper that night, Mother announced the plan to Father as though it were her own. "They will be leaving soon, you know, and we should try to see them while we can."

"That is a good idea. We don't spend enough time with them, and soon we won't be with them at all." Father sighed.

"Elizabeth is looking peaked. I think she is working too hard getting ready for this trip," Mother said, an anxious tone in her voice.

Emily stared at her plate and said nothing. It wasn't her place to tell her parents they would be grandparents before the year was out.

❧

Sunday brought wind and snow. David and Beth walked from the church to the Goodman home, arriving with red cheeks and cold feet.

"Come in!" Father greeted the couple. "Sit by the fire." He pulled two chairs closer to the warming blaze. "Emmy," he called, "do we have some hot tea for these cold people?"

Emily hastened in from the kitchen with a tray of cups and a pot of tea.

"Put it here on this table," Mother ordered. "I will pour it."

"Yes, Mother." Emily gently set down the tray.

"Sit with us, Child," her father urged.

"I have to see to dinner, Father." She hurried back to the kitchen and strained to hear the continuing conversation.

"Well, this weather will slow down the start of your big move," Father told David.

"We have something to tell you," Beth said, taking a deep breath. "We are going to have a baby."

"What?" Mother almost dropped the teapot.

"We've talked to my father," David explained. "He and Jonathan will go on with the plans to leave for New York as soon as the weather permits. Elizabeth and I will follow when the baby is old enough to travel."

"This is wonderful news! A grandchild!" Father clapped his hands together. "Isn't that exciting, Maggie? We'll be grandparents."

Mother sat there, a stunned look on her face. After a moment, she reached for the cups of tea and handed them to her guests, but her lips were set in a thin line.

Father didn't seem to notice. He took the proffered cup and put it on the small table next to his chair. "You've made a good decision to stay here until the baby is born." His face glowed with pleasure. "Emmy, come in here. You need to hear this news," he shouted toward the kitchen.

Emily had been listening at the door. "What's all the fuss?" She caught Beth's glance and winked at her.

"Our Beth is going to have a baby. You will be Aunt Emily," her father boomed.

"Congratulations!" Emmy offered, giving her sister a kiss on the cheek.

"This means we won't be going west for another year," David told the group.

"And your father?" Emmy asked with hope in her heart.

"Father and Jonathan will go as planned. They say they'll be able to get land cleared and cabins built before we come out."

"That makes sense," Father said.

Emily swallowed her hope that Jonathan would stay for another year. What good would it do anyway? *He doesn't know me as anything but Beth's baby sister.*

"How is dinner coming?" Mother interrupted her thoughts.

"Everything is almost ready." Emily scurried back to the kitchen.

"Why isn't Kate here to help?" Beth asked her mother.

"I don't need to pay help when your sister is fully capable of doing the work. It is good for her to learn," Mrs. Goodman said, setting the teapot on the tray with a sharp thud.

"The gristmill does well by us, Margaret. If you need help around the house, hire someone."

"Dinner is ready," Emily called from the kitchen door.

The mood returned to a festive one as talk of the baby flowed. "He will be born in October," Beth told them.

"Have you been to the doctor?" Mother asked.

Beth nodded. "I saw him the first of the week. He says I'm healthy and should have no trouble." She gazed lovingly at her husband. "We'll have a bouncing baby boy."

"Don't be too sure," Mother warned her stern voice. "I only had girls."

"Wonderful girls," Father added. "So what will you do about work, David?"

"I talked to Mr. Richards yesterday. He is glad to have me continue to clerk for him. We'll be able to save more money for supplies before we make the move west."

"Poor Henry thought he would get a job," Mother fussed.

"He seemed delighted not to have to put in more hours when I talked to him yesterday," David said.

Mother smiled at Emily. "Perhaps he will have more time to court you, Dear."

Emily cringed at the thought. "Mother, I don't like him. He is old and—"

"You should be glad someone will look at you," Mother scolded.

"There is nothing wrong with Emmy's looks, Maggie. And she can bake a delicious apple pie." Father took another bite of his dessert.

"Let's go sit in the parlor while the ladies wash up the

dishes, David. I would like to hear more about the land you will be going to and what kind of supplies you'll need."

"You girls do the cleaning up. I have a headache and need to lie down," Mother ordered.

Beth watched Mother walk up the stairs. "Is she sick? She just picked at her food."

"I told you she would not be thrilled at the idea of being a grandmother. She would rather be a grand lady at the top of the social ladder."

"In Ashford? What is she thinking?" Beth carried a stack of dirty plates to the sink.

Emily dipped hot water from the reservoir in the wood-stove into the dishpan. "She isn't happy, but I don't know how to help her."

"It seems to me you work enough. She has you doing all the housework and cooking. What is left for Kate?"

"She does the washing and ironing. Sometimes I wonder why she stays with us. Mother scolds her all the time—worse than she fusses at me."

"Next time I go to the doctor, I'll ask him about Mother. Maybe she has some awful illness."

Emily swished the soap in the hot water and started cleaning the plates. "I'm so ashamed when she yells at Kate that I cover my ears."

"We need to talk to Father about it."

"That will be difficult. I think he sees only what he wants to see. He loves her and seems unwilling to admit to any fault in her."

"It would be nice to have a husband like that."

"You do. David adores you." Emily pushed stray curls off her face with the back of her hand and sighed. "I envy you. So, yes, I am wicked."

"Let's pray about it, Emily. The Lord will show us what to do for Mother."

"And pray she gets over her fixation with Henry Richards.

I will not marry that man."

Beth laughed and dried another plate. "I am glad I'll be home awhile longer."

"Me too," Emily said softly. "It'll be fun to be an aunt. Tomorrow I will start making baby clothes."

"And today, I will start praying for you and Mother."

"Why me?"

"I have to pray Henry Richards out of your life."

The girls laughed as they put the clean dishes on the shelf.

three

Emily stood at her upstairs bedroom window watching Jonathan ride his horse, while his father drove the wagon out of town. Just then he glanced up at her window and tipped his hat. She felt as if her heart would break. *When will I see him again? Will he remember me and come back for me?* Tears spilled down her cheeks. Sighing, she watched until they faded out of sight. *Time will never pass,* she lamented to herself. *I can't wait forever.*

But time passed, and spring turned into the heat of summer. The sun boiled down on Emily as she went to the mercantile for more thread for baby clothes.

"Is Beth all right?" she asked David when he packaged her purchases.

"She's getting as big as a house, and this heat makes her feet swell," David said, looking up quickly. "But I'm not supposed to talk about it."

Emily laughed. "It's all right. I am her sister, and I asked, didn't I?" She held up the soft cloth she had chosen. "This will make fine little garments."

"If you keep this up, we'll need an extra wagon just to carry the little one's wardrobe." He handed her coins in change for her purchases. "We received a long letter from Jonathan. It sounds as if things are going well for him and my father."

Emily didn't remember what else he said. She picked up her package and hurried directly to her sister's. *Did he mention me? Maybe he sent me a message.*

She found Beth sitting in the backyard. "Come and sit down. It's a little cooler here."

19

"David said you got a letter from Jonathan," Emily blurted.

Beth laughed. "And here I thought you came to see me. The letter is on the shelf by the cups in the kitchen. You get it. It's so hot, I refuse to move."

Emily handed the letter to her sister and pulled a chair close to her. "Read it to me."

"Most of it is a list of things for us to take with us. He does write about the Indians."

"Indians? Are they dangerous?" Emily clutched her hands in front of her chest as she pictured Jonathan with an arrow in his chest.

"They might talk us to death." Beth giggled. "Listen to this." She pulled out one of the pages.

> *The red men living in the area are friendly.*
> *One, who calls himself Colonel Dewey, came to*
> *see Pa. It seems he received his commission from*
> *General Washington and fought in the war. When*
> *he heard Pa had met General Washington and*
> *also fought in the war, they became best of*
> *friends. They spend many evenings smoking their*
> *pipes and telling war stories. Colonel Dewey*
> *lives by hunting and fishing. He tells us salmon*
> *will soon fill the creek. Some of his hunting sto-*
> *ries seem a bit far-fetched, but he is a nice man*
> *and a good companion for Pa.*

"What does he write about the land?"

Beth leafed through the pages. "You'll like this part."

> *This is a very pleasant country. There are*
> *many small streams and two little rivers that*
> *flow into the lake. We have found prairies where*
> *game animals abound. There are berry vines,*
> *trees, and chestnuts. Those are still in the husks,*

*but I know they will be the color of Emily's eyes
when they ripen.*

"Oh!" Emily gasped. "He hasn't forgotten me, Beth. I must go with you! I need to be near Jonathan."

Beth reached out to pat her sister. "Why don't I ask Mother to go with me to help with the baby?"

"What! Mother would never do that!"

"You're right. But she won't want to look as if she doesn't care for me, so she'll send you in her place."

"Do you think it will work?"

"Let's start now to plant the seeds and see what happens."

❧

When the autumn leaves turned their burnished gold and bright red, Phillip Miller came into the world. Proudly, David took his son to church to be blessed, and Beth stood at his side trying to keep the kicking infant covered by the small quilt. The Goodmans watched, with the grandfather's face beaming and the grandmother's smile looking more like a grimace. Emily basked in the joy of her sister and brother-in-law.

"What a precious baby," Mrs. Gardner cooed. "You must be so proud, Margaret."

"Of course," Mother murmured.

"It's too bad you're not feeling well enough to go with your daughter," Mrs. Gardner added.

Emily gave Beth a pointed look as their mother assumed what they called her martyred look.

"Yes, we will have to send Emily along when the time comes. She can return home as soon as Elizabeth is settled."

Emily tried to hide her true feelings. If Jonathan wanted to marry her—and she truly hoped he did—she would never come back to Connecticut. *I pray his heart is ready for me.*

With the new baby to fuss over and preparations to complete for the trip, the time went by quickly. Jonathan had written that the trip would be easier if they came by sledge over the snow since the roads were so rough, and David had arranged to rent one for the trip.

After Christmas, when Emily and Beth were having tea, Beth said, "Father has given us a sled and a yoke of oxen. Now we can take more provisions and household goods than we thought."

"What did Mother say?"

"We're not to tell her," Beth said, dropping her voice to a whisper.

"Father said that?" Emily asked in shock.

"I think he sees and hears more than you give him credit for. You don't think Mother is letting you go without his influence, do you?" Beth picked up her cup of tea.

Emily sipped her own tea. "Maybe you're right. I never thought she'd let me go."

Beth smiled triumphantly. "Do you have your trunk packed yet?"

"Yes, and I've packed a small one with some extra clothes. I know you've gone over the lists Jonathan has sent a dozen times, so I'm sure we'll have what we need. Have you set a date?"

"David is looking for a man to go out with us. We need someone to guide us and drive the extra sled."

"I can't wait to go! It will be so exciting!" Emily shivered in anticipation of seeing Jonathan.

"It will be a rough trip in the cold of winter. We may get into storms," Beth warned.

"Are you afraid?" Emily felt sudden concern for her sister.

Beth sighed. "I know this will be a difficult journey, but I'm not afraid. The Lord will take care of us."

ᥫᩗ

In the last week of January, David, Beth, baby Phillip, and Emily climbed aboard the ox-sled. Phineas Davis, who had made the trip with his brother's family a few years earlier, had been hired as guide and the driver of the extra sledge.

"My brother died of the fever a year or more back. I'd like to see how his widow and children are managing on their own," Phineas had explained.

The weather stayed clear and cold. Emily chafed at being tucked into the sled with her sister and the baby. But whenever David thought it safe enough, she would get out and walk beside the oxen.

The first week, they traveled about fifteen miles a day without incident, crossing the Hudson River by scow at Albany. Most nights, they found accommodations in the settlements along the way to Fort Schuyler. After that, the settlements were few and far between.

The second week on the road, the skies turned dark and threatening.

"It's going to storm," Phineas told David from the front sledge where he kept them on the path by following marks on the trees. "We'll have to find a place to stop. I can't see the blazes on the trees in a blizzard."

Emily heard the men talking and looked out from the sheets that had been spread as a cover for the sled. Suddenly, she saw animal tracks in the snow.

"Are those big dogs?" she asked the men.

"No, Miss, they're wolves," Phineas declared.

Emily glanced at her sister. Beth was sleeping. It was just as well she hadn't heard.

"Are they dangerous?"

"Yes, Miss—this time of year they're hungry."

"And we're stopping here?" She shivered, not entirely from the cold.

David had jumped down from the sledge and come back to check on his wife. "Don't frighten her," he told Emily when he saw Beth was asleep. "We'll keep them away from the sleds. You women and the baby can sleep inside."

A short time later, the men found an open spot to spend the night, and Emily climbed out of the sled.

"I'm just going to stretch my legs," she called to her sister, who had awakened when the sled stopped. She made her way through the snow to where David and Phineas were unhooking the oxen. "What can I do to help?" she asked the men.

"Perhaps you can cook us something to eat," David told her. "Make lots of coffee too. It will be a long night."

The men gathered great piles of brush. Beth made sure the baby was comfortable and started helping her sister prepare the meal.

After their simple supper, Emily cleared and repacked the pots while Beth and David were talking. When she had finished, she joined the couple.

"Let's enjoy the fire for awhile, Beth. We can sing some songs." She hoped she could keep her sister distracted. Jonathan hadn't mentioned wolves.

Later, Emily crawled into the sledge with Beth and the baby, but she didn't sleep. She watched as the two men added more wood to keep the fire burning. She had started to doze when she was startled awake by a strange sound. The eerie howl set every nerve in her body quivering. Peering out from the cover, she saw Phineas holding a torch in his hand and waving it toward a shadow. She could hear the menacing growl and see the fire reflecting off the shining white fangs. The animal's yellow eyes gleamed in the firelight. It was not the temperature that froze the blood in her veins. She slept no more that night.

Morning broke in a curtain of white with snow falling in huge blinding flakes.

"Can we go on?" she whispered to Phineas, while David tried to calm his wife.

"We'll try, Miss. If I walked ahead, I could probably find the marks on the trees."

"I've driven horses. I can take your place in the sled," she offered.

David walked up in time to hear her offer. "I'll take the

lead sled. Can you follow me?"

"Yes," Emily said, with more confidence than she felt.

The group moved on. As the snow piled deeper, the way became more difficult. Phineas struggled to find the blazes that marked the path. David and Emily urged the wallowing oxen on through the snowdrifts. In late afternoon, they spotted a light and headed for it, hailing the log cabin with joy. The settlers welcomed them and fed them a hearty meal.

Emily tried to eat the food set in front of her, but exhaustion overcame her. She fell asleep over her meal, rousing only when Beth led her by the arm to the straw mattress they were to share.

In the morning, Emily learned they were close to the end of their journey.

"Mr. Nutting has given us good directions to find our way to Colosse," David said. "Jonathan told us our cabin is only about five miles from there."

"Phillip has been so good," Beth said with a sigh, "but I'll be glad to get to a place of our own. Will Emily have to drive a wagon again today?"

"It'll be clear today, Ma'am, so I can find the way as I drive," Phineas told her. "The new snow is deep, so the oxen will have a bad time getting through."

"Where will we stay tonight?" Emily asked. *I hope I never see another wolf,* she added to herself, shuddering at the thought.

"There's supposed to be a tavern where we can find lodging for the night. It's on our way," David answered.

After thanking the Nuttings, the Miller party traveled on. The snow slowed them, but they did find lodging for the remaining nights.

On the twenty-first day of February they arrived at Rose's Tavern, about a mile from Colosse. After a night there, they rose with anticipation.

Today I will see Jonathan. Emily warmed with the thought.

The day proved an easy one. By midafternoon they reached the cabin they thought belonged to the Millers. Emily didn't wait for the oxen to be unhitched but ran to knock at the door.

When it opened, Emily gasped. There stood a beautiful woman with gentle blue eyes and a riot of red-gold curls, escaping the yarn that held back her long mane of hair.

"Welcome to the Millers'," she greeted Emily.

four

Emily stood in stunned silence and didn't know Beth had come up behind her until the woman at the door asked, "Are you Elizabeth?"

"I am," Beth answered. "And this is my sister, Emily."

"I'm Sally. Won't you come in?" She stepped back, almost stumbling over the little boy who was hiding behind her skirts. Laughing, she put her arm around the child, who looked to be about five years old. "Tommy is shy with strangers."

At the same time, they heard another child crying from the back of the cabin.

"Please sit down." Sally motioned toward the table and benches near the huge fireplace. "I'll get Abbie up, then make us some tea."

Beth urged her sister to sit down on one of the benches. When Phillip heard the other child cry, he started to whimper too.

Emily shook her head sadly, then turned to her sister. "He didn't wait for me," she moaned.

"Now don't you start too," Beth said, glancing at her sister as she tried to quiet her son. "This may not be what you think."

Sally came back with a small girl on her hip. Both the children had the same copper-colored hair and blue eyes as their mother. She spread a quilt in front of the fire and set the toddler down. Tommy sat down next to his sister and watched the newcomers warily.

The young woman pushed the teakettle closer to the fire. "Jonathan and his father are out in the sugar bush. The sap just started to run, and they're tapping the trees. It's going to be a sweet spring with all the maple sugar they'll make." Her infectious laugh made even Emily smile.

The door opened just then, and David and Phineas entered the cabin. Sally stood up at once, a stunned look on her face.

"Phineas?"

"Is that really you, Sally?" he asked, crossing the room and wrapping her in a great hug. "I wondered how I would find you." He stepped back to look at the two children on the quilt. "Are these my niece and nephew?"

"Yes."

Phineas turned to the Millers. "This here is my brother's widow I come to see." Turning back to the young woman, he added, "It looks as if you've managed right well."

Sally Davis looked down at her children. "We were near starving when Mr. Miller came to our rescue about a year ago. We'd been living on boiled fish and johnnycake."

"I didn't hear about Tom's death until last summer," Phineas told her.

"Let me make some tea for all of us, and I'll tell you what happened." She turned to the shelf on the wall opposite the table and took down a teapot and a canister.

Emily watched but said nothing. She said Mr. Miller found her. *Maybe she isn't Jonathan's woman.* Hope began to come back into her heart.

When they were seated around the table with mugs of tea and the children were playing on the quilt, Sally turned to Phineas. "Your brother had taken our corn to Rotterdam to the grist mill. He came back with a fever. It raged through him, taking all his strength. Polly Wheeler does the nursing around here, and she came. But there was nothing we could do. He was dead within a week." She stopped to wipe away a tear. "He had wood in for the winter, but we didn't have enough fodder for the ox. I had dried some berries and vegetables and salted a barrel of fish. I was near my time with Abigail and couldn't do any more. I let the ox loose, and the poor thing fed on tree limbs that winter. Polly has four sons, and she sent Rufus, the middle one, to stay with me when the baby was due."

"Rover?" asked Tommy, looking up from where he was playing.

"Yes, he brought his dog, Rover too, didn't he, Son?"

Sally took a sip of tea. "When my water broke, Rufus went for his mother. It was dark, and he took the lantern. But he fell trying to run in the snow. The candle went out, and he couldn't get it lit again. He said he took hold of the dog's tail and told Rover to go home. That old dog led him to the Wheeler cabin. Polly came at first light. By that time, Abigail had been born, and I had cut the cord."

She put an arm around Tommy who had come to stand by his mother's side. "Luckily this one slept through it all."

Looking at the others around the table she continued. "Polly got the baby and me cleaned up and made us a pot of stew." She sighed. "That was about Christmastime. It was a long, hard winter, and we were down to a few pieces of salt fish and a couple of pounds of cornmeal when Mr. Miller knocked on our door. He wondered who the ox belonged to." She picked up her cup. "And that's how I come to be here. He's a good Christian man and took the children and me in."

Phineas looked embarrassed. "I came as soon as I could. Mr. Miller," he said, nodding toward David, "rented a sled and a pair of oxen. I'm to bring them back, and I thought, if I could find you and the children, I'd offer to take you back east."

"You're kind, Phineas, but I have nothing to go back to. I want to try to hold on to the land Tom and I bought together."

Sally looked at the sisters huddled together on the bench. "It would be too crowded now with all of us here. I'll be moving back to my own cabin as soon as the men are finished with the maple sugar. It'll be near time to put in a garden by then."

"Won't they come home tonight?" Emily ventured to ask.

Sally smiled and shook her head. "They have a shed where

they keep a fire going all the time for the sap to boil down. Colonel Dewey helps some, but mostly it's the two of them who take turns sleeping, feeding the fire, and emptying sap buckets."

"That's the Indian Jonathan wrote about," Emily said.

"Colonel Dewey is teaching Mr. Miller and Jonathan how to make the syrup, sugar, then molasses from the sap. He and Mr. Miller are good friends."

"Where is the shed?" David asked. "I'd like to go out and see my father and brother."

"I have a pot of stew, and I baked johnnycake yesterday. I had planned to take it to the men today. I'll get things together and take you to them."

"Will your children stay with us?" Beth asked.

"I usually pull them on a small sled Jonathan made, but I think they'll stay with you."

Tommy glanced from one to the other. Beth had put Phillip on the quilt with Abigail, who stopped sucking her thumb to watch the baby kick and squeal.

"Will you take care of Abbie for a little while?" Sally asked the boy.

He nodded his head and went to sit by his sister.

"I'll start bringing some of the things in from the sled," Phineas said. "We'll put the oxen out by the barn. There isn't room for all of them inside—but they've been outside most nights since we've been on the road anyway."

Sally took her cloak down from a peg at the back of the cabin. "You'll find some room for provisions in the corner back there." She pointed to the alcove opposite the bed where Abbie had been sleeping. "It's only a little over a mile to the sugar bush, so we won't be gone long. Maybe Mr. Miller will come back and tell you where he wants things."

"What can we do to help you?" Beth got up from the bench.

"You can put your quilts on the bed. I have a straw mattress the children and I can sleep on."

"I don't want to put you out of your bed," Beth protested.

Sally smiled. "It isn't mine. It was supposed to be for you when you came. The men sleep in the loft and have let me use the bed down here until you arrived." She turned to Emily. "We'll put together another mattress for you, and we'll sleep by the fire." With that, she took up a pot of stew and a pan of bread and led David out the door.

"Do you feel better now?" Beth asked Emily after Phineas had also gone outside.

"Beth, she's beautiful. Jonathan won't even see me now."

"She's too old for him. He will be glad to see you. Just you wait and see." She hugged her sister. "Now let's see what Phineas is pulling out of the sled." She looked around the cabin. "Where will we put all the things we brought, plus all these people?"

"I thought Jonathan wrote that they were building two cabins," Emily said as she opened the door for Phineas, who carried in a pile of quilts.

"Yes, but. . ." A giggled erupted from Beth. "Oh, Emily, can you imagine Mother in a place like this?"

Emily laughed with her sister. Feeling better, she sat down with the children and started to tickle the fussy Phillip.

Great mounds of goods started to fill the corner Sally had indicated to Phineas. "I see the sack of wheat flour," Emily said. "Maybe I can bake some biscuits to go with Sally's stew."

"What will you use for an oven?" Beth asked.

Emily looked at the huge fireplace. "I have no idea."

"I think I saw a reflector oven under the shelf. Do you want me to show you how to use it?" Phineas asked.

Emily smiled at the man. "It's the first of many things I must learn about this place. Now, what is a reflector oven?"

By the time they heard Sally outside, Emily's first reflector-oven biscuits were baking. She watched them closely, though, knowing they could easily burn. She didn't look up when the door opened—not until she heard his voice.

Standing up quickly, she looked into the warm blue eyes of the man she had traveled all this way to see. She tried to speak his name, but her mouth was too dry to make a sound.

"Emily," Jonathan said quietly, looking into her eyes.

In that moment, without a word or a touch, Emily sensed her life was bound to this man's.

"Your biscuits are burning," Phineas said.

"Oh!" Emily knelt down on the hearth to pull the pan back from the reflected heat.

"We brought back some of the first syrup. Over biscuits it will be the sweetest treat you ever tasted," Sally declared. "Are those made with wheat flour? I haven't tasted wheat flour in years." She hugged Emily. "You're a dear to make them for us."

"Here's the syrup," Jonathan said, as he extended a jug toward Emily.

All else in the room faded as Emily searched his face. She felt as if they were alone in their own world. He returned her steady gaze until Sally took the jug from his hand, breaking the breathtaking moment.

The evening went by quickly as Jonathan told them some of the things he and his father had accomplished. "I'll go back to the sugar bush tomorrow with the augurs David brought. We can tap a lot more trees now."

"What will you do with all the sugar and syrup? We can't use all that," Beth said.

"We take it to Fort Ontario at Oswego. We can sell or trade it there for things we need. They have ships traveling back and forth between Quebec and Oswego, and they'll take trade goods. Father and I went there last fall to get supplies for the winter."

"Did you sell ashes like your father said?" Beth asked.

Jonathan smiled. "Yes, we did. They make glass in Quebec and need the potash. We got our nine cents a barrel with no trouble and met our interest payments with a little extra."

Phillip started to fuss again. "He's hungry," Beth said, taking the baby back to the bed to nurse him in private.

"It's been a long day for me," Phineas declared. "I'm going to get some sleep." He climbed the ladder to the loft.

Sally had put her mattress by the fire. Tommy and Abbie were already asleep. "I'll get ready to join the children," she said, heading back to where Beth fed Phillip.

"I prayed you would find a way to come with David and Beth," Jonathan told Emily. "After I left Ashford, on the long journey out here, I remembered seeing you standing in the upstairs window of your house. I couldn't get that picture of you out of my mind. I'm so glad you have come."

"I didn't think my mother would allow it. She let me come to help Beth, but she wants me to come right back home."

He looked stricken. "Will you go back with Phineas?"

Emily shook her head. "No, I told Mother I would stay until Beth got settled." She didn't add that she would stay forever if he wanted her to.

"I hope Beth needs you for many years," he said with a chuckle. "I know I will," he added in a whisper Emily wasn't sure she heard or imagined.

five

At first light, the women were up sorting through the piles of goods in the corner.

"Oh, look!" Sally exclaimed.

Emily watched Sally's work-worn hands smooth the bolt of calico she had found.

"David worked in the mercantile in Ashford. When we left, the owner gave us that cloth," Beth explained.

With her finger, Sally traced the blue flowers on the cream-colored background. "I love blue flowers," she said wistfully. "I guess I'm too used to sewing things out of salt sacks." She put the calico on the pile of goods to be stored in the loft.

"Here's the featherbed I brought. I'll make up the bed here with it." Beth pulled the mattress out of the stack.

"Save the old mattress to take back to Sally's cabin," Jonathan told them.

"Why?" Sally asked in a puzzled tone.

"Squirrels have been nesting in the one that's there."

"You went by there?" Sally asked.

"When I'm hunting, I check in from time to time. We'll need to clean it up before you move back."

"Why don't I plan to stay there till I start back east? I can keep the fire going and dry the place out," Phineas offered.

"That sounds good, Phineas. You girls pick out what you want to go over there, and we'll get started," Jonathan instructed.

"What about these augurs and buckets? Your father will need them in the sugar bush," Sally said.

"Can you drive one sled out there while we take the other

to your cabin?" Jonathan asked.

With the decision made, everyone started working to load the two sleds.

"May I go with you?" Emily asked Jonathan.

"We can take Phineas over to Sally's to stay, then you and I will bring the sled back here."

"What will I do?" Beth looked about the room at the others.

"Let's bundle up the children and go out to where they're boiling syrup. Maybe some sugar will be ready for them to taste," Sally said.

"Can I go see Papa?" Tommy asked in excitement.

Emily glanced at her sister when the child referred to Mr. Miller as Papa. Beth raised her eyebrows but said nothing.

By the middle of the morning the sleds were packed. Jonathan banked the fire in the cabin, and they set off in two directions. Emily sat close to him on the seat, while Phineas found a place in the sled.

"It is more beautiful than you described in your letters," she told Jonathan. "Did your apple trees grow?"

"They did well last summer. We'll have to wait to see if they survive the winter."

"Do you plan to plant more?"

"I have some seeds growing in the cabin. We'll plant them when the ground warms up," Jonathan told her as he steered the oxen around a snow bank.

"Someday you'll have a big orchard."

"Maybe, but it's a hard life here for both trees and people. There isn't always bright sunshine sparkling on the snow. The weather can be harsh."

She glanced at him and saw in his eyes that he would like to be there for her no matter what storms blew around them.

"Learning to live here will be exciting. We did so much to prepare for the trip. Beth and I sewed stacks of quilts with endless rows of tiring stitches. We must have enough quilts for three families."

"That's good, because it looks as if we'll have three families."

"What do you mean?"

"My pa dotes on Sally's children. Didn't you hear Tommy call him 'Papa'? When the boy started that, I thought my father would burst with joy. He takes the boy fishing and plays with Abigail, and," he added, grinning at her, "Sally is a beautiful woman."

"He's a lot older," Emily pointed out.

"True, but out here, Sally doesn't have much choice."

"How can they get married here? There isn't any church."

Jonathan clucked to the oxen to move them along faster. "We have a preacher who comes around. When the weather permits, we gather at different houses and read the Bible. We call it our Fellowship of Faith. We talk about the Scriptures and try to encourage each other." He looked at Emily. "I'm sure, when the preacher comes around again, my pa and Sally will get married."

I wonder if we will get married. She felt her face flush at the thought. *He hasn't asked me yet, so I must wait and see.*

Just then, Jonathan pulled the oxen to a stop by a small cabin. "You might want to do some cleaning. Do you mind?"

"I can clean better than I can use a reflector oven." Emily laughed as he lifted her down from the seat.

Phineas hopped out of the back. "Nice spot here." He walked around to the back of the cabin.

Emily followed Jonathan through the door. Furry bodies fled into corners. "Leave the door open, and we'll shoo them out," he told her. "The squirrels can find another place to live."

Emily found a homemade broom and started sweeping at the back corner of the small cabin, trying to round up the squirrels.

"Phineas, can you get a fire going? Maybe this old straw mattress the animals have been tearing up will make good starter," Jonathan suggested.

"There's still some cut wood out back. We should have a

fire roaring in a few minutes." Phineas carried logs to the fireplace. "Then I'm going to clean up my brother's gun and see if I can shoot a deer."

With the broom, Emily reached under the bunk where the old mattress had been. "Those squirrels lived well. Look at all the nut shells!"

"Sally has black walnut trees nearby," Jonathan informed her. He took the broom from her and pushed the shells from under the bed.

The three worked until late afternoon. Jonathan brought pails of water from the stream for Emily to heat, and she scrubbed the shelves and dishes. Phineas killed a deer and hung some of the venison in the lean-to outside.

"There'll be meat for me to eat while I'm here, and you can take the rest back to the Miller cabin. You'll have more people to feed there."

"How long will you stay?" Emily asked him.

"No more than three or four days. I have to get started while there's still snow for the sled. Mr. Miller has wheels to put on his sled, but I only have heavy runners." He looked around the cabin. "You got it cleaned up real good. I know Sally will appreciate it."

"Jonathan is still patching the roof. Then we'll go back. I left you johnnycake, cornmeal, and some leftover stew." Emily showed him where she had stored the food.

"I won't starve. It bothers me that Tom's wife nearly did." He hesitated. "I had hoped she'd go back with me. She's a good woman."

Jonathan entered the cabin then. "I think that roof will hold out the weather. Do you want us to come back for you in a few days?"

"No, I'm much obliged, but it isn't far. And I saw the old blazes on the trees, so I won't get lost." He shook Jonathan's hand. "Thank you for taking care of my sister-in-law."

"It's my father who found her and has been caring for her."

He looked around the small room. "He's talking about adding a room come summer. They'll be needing a barn too. He wants to have a cow so the children will have milk."

"I'm grateful to God that she has a good family. Sally's folks are gone, so besides me, she doesn't have anyone."

Jonathan put his hand on Phineas's shoulder. "She'll be well cared for now."

❧

"Sally is so pretty I thought you might care for her," Emily admitted on the ride back to the Miller cabin.

Jonathan chuckled. "No, I prefer hair and eyes the color of chestnuts."

Emily felt her cheeks grow warm in the frosty air. "Beth read me that letter. It was when we started trying to get Mother to let me come out with Beth and David." She went on to tell Jonathan how they had convinced their mother that Beth needed help and how when her mother didn't want to make the trip, she had decided to send Emily.

"And now that you are here, how will you convince her to let you stay?" Jonathan asked in genuine concern.

"I'm still hoping for an answer to that," Emily answered quietly with true longing in her heart, but her thoughts turned to her father, who was left alone to face her mother's wrath. She prayed that she had made the right decisions and that God would be with him.

Emily entered the cabin, while Jonathan tended to the oxen. The children's cheeks were red from their day in the outdoors.

Tommy tugged on her skirt. "I brought you a present." He held out a lump of maple sugar.

Emily bent down on her knees to give the boy a hug. "You brought this for me?"

"I have competition," Jonathan complained in a mock growl, coming through the door. He whisked the boy into the air and laughed when Tommy squealed.

Putting the child down he turned to Sally. "How are my

father and brother doing?"

"Your father was energized by the introduction to his grandson, but the men will need your help in boring the extra augurs into the trees. It'll take all of you working round the clock to keep the buckets emptied and the sap boiling." She smiled. "It's going to be a good sap season."

"I'll leave at first light. I'm hungry now. When do you think supper will be ready?"

Sally turned to Emily. "Would you like to learn how to cook with a spider?"

"You cook spiders?" Horror filled Emily as she remembered all the spiders she had swept out of Sally's cabin earlier in the day.

Sally's rich laugh filled the air. "No, we don't cook spiders! We cook in one. You learned about the reflector oven yesterday; now let me teach you to make johnnycake in this." She took a large cast-iron frying pan off the shelf and showed her the foot-like appendages on the bottom of the pan.

"First you mix a cup of cornmeal and a bit of salt, and tonight we can add a spoon of sugar, since we have some. Then add a cup and a half of boiling water. That's your batter. Now you pull some coals out of the fire." She did this, showing Emily how the four feet on the spider sat over the coals. "When it's hot, you drop spoonfuls of batter on the pan and fry it." She looked wistful. "It will be nice when we have bacon fat to cook them in."

"The pigs aren't born yet, and you're cooking them already," Jonathan teased. "When I had the stump mill going, I ground cornmeal for the Wheeler family. They owe me two pigs out of their sow's next litter," he explained to Beth and Emily.

"Phineas sent us venison. How do you cook that?" Emily asked.

"We can cut it up into the stew pot and add a little water," Sally said, "then let it simmer."

"If I burn the johnnycake the way I did the biscuits, we can soak it in the gravy," Emily said, smiling.

"Tomorrow we'll do a week's baking. Do you see this?" Sally opened the iron door at the side of the fireplace. "Jonathan built this when he built the fireplace. We fill the inside with wood," she said, pointing to the space built into the rock. "When the wood burns down, we pull out the ashes and put our baking in. When the door is closed, the rocks hold the heat and bake whatever we put inside."

"Could we roast a chunk of that venison and take it out to the men?" Beth asked.

"That's a good idea," Sally agreed.

"With three cooks, I expect some special meals," Jonathan said, pouring himself a cup of tea from the pot on the hearth.

"And you'll get them too—no need to worry!" Sally smiled at the young man, then turned to Beth and Emily. "I need to get busy knitting. We have an endless need for socks and mittens around here." Her yawn ended in a grin. The day in the cold air, then a good meal had made even the adults sleepy. "But I'll start tomorrow. Right now I'm ready to join the children." She pointed to her little ones curled up asleep on the mattress by the fire.

"I'll leave as soon as I have light enough to see," Jonathan told the women.

Emily felt her heart sadden. *I want to be with him everyday. He'll be a lot closer than he was before, though, and he'll be back in a few days,* she reminded herself.

"We'll cook tomorrow and bring food out the next day if the weather is good," Sally told him.

Jonathan looked deep into Emily's eyes for a moment before he climbed the ladder to the loft. Tired as she was, she lay awake thinking until at last she fell asleep.

six

Emily sat up with a start.

"It's all right. I wanted to build up the fire and light a lantern," Jonathan whispered.

"But it's still night," she protested, clutching her quilt around her neck.

"It'll be light soon. I need the lantern so I can see to hook up the oxen." Taking a burning twig from the fireplace, he opened the side of the lantern and lit the candle inside.

"I'll fix you something to eat." Emily started to get up.

"No, let the others sleep. Pa will have hot coffee and johnny-cake." He knelt beside her, searching her face as if trying to save it in his memory for the days ahead.

"When will you be back?" she asked quietly.

"We'll take turns bringing in the jugs of syrup and boxes of sugar. I'll see you in a few days." His voice was husky, then he disappeared into the darkness.

Emily lay back down but did not sleep. She prayed for Jonathan and the others who were working so hard to harvest the maple syrup.

By the time the children stirred, the sky had lightened to a dull gray.

"Looks like a storm is brewing," Sally said, carrying in an armload of wood. She filled the oven with kindling and lit it with coals from the fireplace.

"Will you need more wood?" Emily asked.

"Yes, it takes a lot to fill this up. As soon as we get a bed of coals, we'll stack the oven full. Jonathan built in a good draft, so it burns fine." She sighed. "I'll miss this when I go back to my reflector oven in the cabin."

41

"Maybe Jonathan will build you one."

"His father built me an outdoor oven last summer. It's nice when the weather gets hot."

"Jonathan said his pa plans to add a room to your cabin," Emily said, dropping more wood by the oven. She watched Sally's pale face turn bright red.

"We've talked about it," the young woman said quietly.

"David's father is a fine man," Beth said, joining the conversation. "He's been very good to me since David and I married. I was afraid he would be upset when David didn't come out with him last year."

Sally smiled. "He talked a lot about being a grandfather. I think he wanted to be sure I knew how old he was."

"Does it matter?" Emily asked, ignoring her sister's warning look.

Sally sighed and shook her head. "I feel God sent him to take care of the children and me. I'm thankful for my blessings."

Emily and Sally set about mixing cornmeal bread batter, while Beth prepared a roast of venison.

"The end of the sap run makes good molasses. Won't it be wonderful to cook beans with molasses? Jonathan and his father arrived here at the end of the sap run last year, so I haven't had molasses in at least two years," Sally told the sisters.

"I know we'll grow more beans, but Father insisted we bring a fifty-pound bag of dry beans out with us," Beth said, swinging the hanging pot over the coals to boil water.

"It will be a few months before we harvest anything from our garden. I'm glad Father gave us so much. I only hope Mother never finds out."

"Emmy, you are too harsh about Mother," Beth scolded. "She had a hard childhood and is afraid of not having enough."

"She lives like a queen. Why is she so against sharing? She didn't even want to share with her own daughters."

Beth sighed as she stirred beans into the pot. "Maybe she thinks we have it too easy and should suffer as she did."

"Let's invite her out," Emily said, a trace of bitterness in her voice. "I can just see her cooking over a fireplace."

"When your last letter came, Jonathan mentioned about your parents and said he doubted they would let Emily come. He said he might build his cabin and go back to Ashford, to ask you to come back with him," Sally told Emily.

The words brought a glow to Emily. *He had wanted to come back for me!*

"Now we have to convince Mother to let Emily stay," Beth told Sally.

Emily shuddered. She didn't miss her mother at all, but once again, her thoughts turned to her father. She missed his warm hugs, but she was sure that he would wish for Emily to be happy wherever that may lead her.

The cabin filled with heat and good smells as the food cooked. While she was setting the table, Emily watched Phillip lying contentedly on the quilt on the floor. The next time she turned to look, he had rolled over and was crawling to Abbie, who promptly grabbed at his toes when he reached her. Meanwhile, Tommy was playing with the wooden animals Mr. Miller had carved for him.

The cozy family scene filled Emily with a sense of contentment.

&

The storm moved in, and heavy snow fell most of the night. "We won't be able to take food to the men," Beth said the next morning.

"I can get through," Sally declared. "I won't try to take the oxen. I'll pull the sled Jonathan made for the children. We can bundle up the food and tie it on that."

"Can you find your way?" Emily asked.

"The road is marked, and we've been over it so much you can see the ruts even with new snow."

Emily and Beth prepared the meat, corn bread, and beans, while Sally wrapped her cloak around her body and a scarf around her head and lower face.

"I'll be back before dark," she promised.

Emily and Beth watched their new friend disappear into the swirling snow.

"I pray she makes it safe," Emily said.

"Amen," Beth added. She shut the door and turned to her sister. "Whatever possessed you to ask Sally about Mr. Miller's age? You embarrassed me."

"They're going to get married."

"Really? How do you know that?"

"Jonathan told me the day we went to clean her cabin. His father already has plans to enlarge her cabin and buy a cow so the children can have milk."

"Well, he has been widowed a long time. It would be nice for him to have a woman to look after him."

"Beth, did you see the way she looked at the bolt of calico?"

"Yes," Beth answered, a puzzled look on her face.

"Why don't we sew her a new dress to get married in?"

"Oh, that's a wonderful idea!" her sister exclaimed. "But won't they have to go to one of the settlements to find a preacher?"

"Jonathan says a preacher comes here sometimes. He's sure the next time he shows up, his father and Sally will get married."

"I've heard about the fellowship meetings they have. I guess I didn't understand that a preacher comes to them sometimes. Did Jonathan suggest you be part of the wedding too?" Beth asked with a twinkle in her eyes.

Emily felt her face burn. "No, he didn't," she said quietly, then looked at her sister. "He did ask me if I knew how to get Mother to let me stay longer."

Just then Phillip started to cry, and Beth hurried to pick up her son. Later that afternoon when Phillip and Abbie were taking naps, Emily and Beth took down Sally's extra dress and started to take measurements.

"What are you doing to Mommy's dress?" Tommy asked.

"Can you keep a secret?" Emily asked the little boy.

He looked bewildered.

Emily knelt down in front of Tommy. "Miss Beth and I want to surprise your mommy. We thought we would make her a new dress. You won't tell, will you?"

Tommy's face beamed. "Can I tell Papa?"

"No, this will be a surprise for him too."

"I won't tell anyone," the little boy promised solemnly.

"We can work on this after she moves back to her cabin," Beth said.

It was nearly dark, and Sally had not returned to the Miller cabin. The two sisters had started to worry.

"We don't even know where to start looking," Beth fretted.

But just then Sally came through the door, covered in snow.

"Are you all right?" Emily hurried to her side.

"I fell. I'm not hurt, but I am cold and tired. Do you have any hot tea?"

Beth had already taken a mug from the shelf and started to fill it.

"Let me take your cloak. I'll hang it on a peg near the fire." Emily helped Sally remove her snow-covered clothes.

"It was a long trip in the new snow. I had to walk through drifts of two and three feet. But I made it." She sat on a bench and took the cup Beth offered.

"The men were pleased to have the food. They don't have much time to cook more than a pot of coffee or boil some tea." She sipped the hot drink in front of her. "The sap is running good. They say they'll get about three to five pounds of sugar from every tree they've tapped."

"That's a lot of sugar!" Emily exclaimed.

"Jonathan says he should have made more boxes. He made a stack of them this winter to keep the sugar in."

"How much longer will they tap the trees?" Beth asked.

"Well, they've been at it a couple of weeks—maybe a week or ten days more." Sally put her arm around Tommy. "You look happy. Did you have fun today?"

The boy grinned from ear to ear and nodded, glancing at Emily as he did.

"Look what I have for you." Sally reached into her pocket and brought out a carved horse. "Papa sent it to you."

"Oh, he looks like Jonathan's mare!" the boy cried with pleasure.

Sally looked at the sisters. "Did someone feed and water the animals?"

"I did," Emily assured her. "Their water was frozen, so I got some from the creek."

"I like having the well under the house. We don't have to find an open spot in the creek," Beth said. "We just open the trap door and lower a bucket."

"More of Jonathan's ideas," Sally said. "He's already dug a well under his cabin."

The next day the snow stopped falling, and the sun shone brightly. Tommy went with Emily to help with the stock.

"I didn't tell Mommy," he said in a whisper.

Emily hugged him. "You're a good boy, and we'll be able to surprise your mother." Emily was piling wood on her arm to take back to the cabin when Phineas hailed them.

"I thought I'd better get back here before it stormed again. I brought you some rabbits," he said, showing them the animals he carried on a stick over his shoulder.

"Come in and warm up," Emily told him, taking the rabbits. "I'll skin these and fry them for supper."

After the women had cleared away the supper dishes, Sally sat down with her knitting. "I'd better start thinking about getting back to my place."

"I kept the fire going so it should be dried out. Don't wait too long, or the squirrels will move back in." Phineas chuckled.

"How soon do you have to leave, Phineas?" Beth asked.

"In a day or two. I'll keep an eye on the weather. You know there's a stretch where we didn't find accommodations. I don't want to get stuck out in a blizzard again." He grinned. "I won't have Miss Emily to drive the oxen for me this time."

"If I get my things together, will you take the sled by my place?" Sally asked.

"I'd be glad to. I cut some more wood too."

Tommy pushed up against Emily's side. "I want to stay here."

Sally put her knitting needles down. "Don't you want to go home with Abbie and me?"

Tommy looked confused. "I want to be here when Papa comes home."

"Why don't you let Tommy stay with us until the men come back? Mr. Miller will bring him over to you and check to make sure you're all right," Emily suggested as she hugged Tommy.

"I don't feel right asking you to take care of him."

"Tommy is my helper," Emily declared. "He helps me feed and water the animals."

"Well, I am leaving you work there too. I don't plan to take my ox back until there's feed in the field for him. I don't have any grain or hay at my place."

Phineas laughed. "If you did, the deer would have eaten it. They're all around your place. You can shoot all the meat you'll need."

"I never did learn to shoot that gun. Why don't you take your brother's gun back with you, Phineas? Tom would have wanted you to have it." She picked up her knitting when she noted the look of pleasure on her brother-in-law's face.

"Jonathan will be hunting and will keep Sally in meat. If we tell him about the deer there, he'll go and shoot one for her," Emily told Phineas.

"You'll have to tell him. I'll be on my way back east, but I'm mighty pleased to have my brother's gun."

"Papa takes me hunting sometimes," Tommy said with pride.

"Well, if Papa Miller goes to hunt by your mother's cabin he can take you to visit her."

"I'd like that," the child said and looked at his mother. "Can I stay here? I'll come home when Papa says I should."

Sally smiled. "I don't have much choice, do I?" She tousled her son's bright curls.

In two days, Sally had packed what she needed into the sledge. She and Phineas said their good-byes and left. Tommy looked sad when his mother faded out of sight, but Emily took his hand and led him back into the cabin.

"Let's go find that pretty cloth to start your mother's new dress."

They were in the loft when they heard Jonathan's voice.

"Is Papa with you?" Tommy scrambled down the ladder and ran to the door.

Jonathan and David came in the door. "He didn't come this time, but next time he'll be home to stay," David said, crossing the room to pick up his son and greet his wife.

Jonathan swung Tommy up high on his shoulder. "How come you are here and your sister is gone?"

"Miss Emily and I have a secret, and I'm not going to tell."

Jonathan looked at Emily and smiled. "Do I get to know about this?"

"Not yet," Emily told him. "How long can you stay?"

"Only long enough to unload the sled and feed the oxen. We'll take the sled back. We have so much sugar and syrup to bring in that we need it."

He put the boy back on the floor. "We'll take some food back, if you have any to spare."

"Phineas brought rabbits, and we have some extra. He just left this morning to move Sally back to her place. Then he'll be on his way back east."

Jonathan looked at her and said quietly, "I'm glad you didn't go with him."

seven

Emily felt warm inside at his words. "I sent a letter with Phineas. I didn't tell my parents about the blinding blizzard or the starving wolves. But I told them how you men have to be away days at a time, tapping the maple trees and making sugar and syrup. My reason for staying is so Beth won't be left alone in the wilderness."

Jonathan laughed. "It sounds convincing to me. I hope your mother agrees and you can stay."

Why doesn't he ask me to stay as his wife?

"Be patient," an inner voice told Emily. *"You have just learned he wanted to come back for you. He may want to be sure you can live on the frontier."*

"How are you and Beth getting along without Sally?" he asked, as if reading her thoughts.

"We're doing fine." She reached down and hugged Tommy to her side. "This young man helps me feed and water the stock."

The little boy's face beamed, and he asked wistfully, "When will Papa come back? I want to see him."

"Tommy stayed here so he would get to see your father when he comes back," Emily explained.

"Why don't I take him back with us?"

Tommy's eyes grew big and round. He looked up at Emily. "Can I go? Please, can I go to see Papa?"

Jonathan tousled Tommy's hair. "Pa is working too hard. If Tommy is there, maybe he'll ease off a bit and let David and me do more work. We'll have more sugar and syrup to bring back here in a day or two. Tommy and Pa can bring it in."

Emily hesitated a moment, but she couldn't refuse the

longing in the boy's eyes. "I'll get some warm clothes and a quilt for him."

She gathered up the things Tommy would need. *How gentle Jonathan is. He will be a good father to our children.* She could feel her face grow warm at the thought.

"Here are the rabbits and some corn bread," Beth said, helping her husband bundle food to take back to their sugar camp. "I hope you come back to stay soon."

The note of longing in her sister's voice did not escape Emily's ears, and she gave silent assent as she watched Jonathan lift Tommy into the sled.

★

Emily and Beth worked that day and the next on the dress for Sally.

"Do you think she will like it?" Beth asked.

"Didn't you see the look on her face when she saw the calico? I think she'll be overjoyed. I wonder when the preacher will make his rounds."

"Do you want a double wedding?" Beth teased her sister.

"I don't know what to think. Jonathan has talked about my staying, but he never suggests I stay as his wife."

Beth patted her sister's hand. "I don't know exactly how men think. But he may take for granted you will marry now that you are here."

"I would feel a lot better if he would speak it."

Beth looked up from her work. "I hear the oxen coming!"

Quickly they gathered up their sewing and hid it under the quilt on Beth's bed.

"Papa and me brought the syrup in. Can you make some biscuits to go with it?" Tommy asked, bursting into the cabin.

"Just like a man.," Emily laughed. "He's always thinking of his stomach." She scooped the little boy into her arms. "Did you help make the syrup?"

He nodded his head. "I carried lots of wood to keep the fire going. "Mr. David said they are getting down to the molasses and vinegar time now."

"Vinegar too?" Beth asked her father-in-law as he entered the cabin.

"The late sap makes good vinegar. We'll be able to put down a crock of pickles in the fall," Mr. Miller told her. "Now let me see that grandson of mine. His father has kept me working too hard these last few days to come and play with this young addition to the Miller clan."

Emily watched Tommy, but he did not seem jealous of the baby. Instead, he insisted on telling Papa Miller all the things the baby could do. "Abbie likes to play with him too," he told the older man.

"We'll let David and Jonathan keep the sap boiling, and tomorrow we'll go and see your mother and your little sister," Mr. Miller said, keeping an arm around Tommy while holding Phillip.

"Let me get you a cup of coffee," Beth said as her father-in-law carried the baby to a bench to sit down.

"I'm hungry," Tommy announced.

"I'd better start those biscuits. Maybe I can bake them without burning them this time." Emily smiled and reached for the sack of wheat flour.

The morning brought a warm breeze. "The snow will melt fast if this keeps up," Mr. Miller predicted. "We'll take the Indian cart to your mother's," he told Tommy, who sat close to the man while he ate the cornmeal mush and maple syrup.

"What is an Indian cart?" Emily asked, pouring more coffee.

"Indians taught us to make them—that's where the name comes from. Basically, we used a pole with a crook at the end. Where the ends are separated we made a seat and fastened the pole end to the yoke of an ox. You girls can use it to go visiting. That's the fashionable way to travel," he told the sisters with a grin.

"I can show you," Tommy said.

"I'll watch you and Papa Miller hook this rig up so I know

how to do it the next time," Emily said.

"Can we shoot a deer?" the boy asked.

"I'll take the rifle along. We can lash venison on the seat and walk back beside the cart. When David and Jonathan get back, they can fire up the smokehouse and make jerky."

"Mommy can do that," Tommy spoke with pride.

"She must teach us," Beth said, then turned to her father-in-law. "How much longer before David comes back?"

"Not more than a week," he assured her.

Another week, thought Emily, with a sigh.

⁂

The sugar bush camp was finally closed at the end of March. The boxes and jugs of maple syrup were stored in the root cellar Jonathan had dug next to the cabin.

"We'll have a good load to take to Fort Ontario to trade," Jonathan told Emily.

"When will you go?" Emily asked, dreading his leaving again.

"Not for a few weeks. The snow is melting, and the mud will make travel difficult for awhile."

The softness of his voice and the warmth in his eyes as he looked at her made Emily's heart beat faster.

"We left some of the equipment at the sugar bush," Mr. Miller reminded his sons. "We should bring it back here while we can still use the sled. The snow is melting fast."

"Emily and I can go out in the morning and be back with all the gear in the afternoon," Jonathan offered.

"The mare needs some exercise about now. Maybe Tommy and I will ride her over to Sally's tomorrow," his father said.

Emily felt the excitement of a proposed day with Jonathan. *We never get to talk to each other around here.* She looked at her sister and David and felt guilty that she thought of time alone with Jonathan. David and Beth had had almost no time together since arriving at the cabin.

The next morning dawned bright, full of blue sky and

sunshine. Tommy could hardly wait to eat breakfast before getting the mare out and starting for his mother's.

Jonathan hitched the oxen to the sledge and helped Emily onto the seat. She turned to see her sister standing next to David and holding Phillip. Both were waving to Emily and Jonathan.

"David has been away a lot since we got here. I think Beth was getting lonely," Emily told Jonathan as they started along the rutted path.

"This life isn't the same as when he would come home from the store every night. Do you think she'll get used to it?"

"She's a strong woman and loves her husband very much. I can't ever think of her regretting the move to the frontier," Emily said with conviction.

"She would miss you if you went back east," Jonathan said, glancing at her.

"I have no intention of going back." Emily could have bit her tongue for speaking so bluntly. "I mean, I'll stay as long as she needs me."

The sledge hit a muddy spot in the road, and the oxen strained to move along again. "The snow will be gone soon. Then I can get back to working on my cabin."

"Do you have a lot to do?" Emily wanted to know more about this cabin. *Will it be my home?*

"Yes, I've dug the well and put the walls up. But when we got the stump mill going last fall, I spent all my time grinding corn."

"What is the stump mill? My father has a gristmill with stones."

"Maybe someday we'll have one of those. Right now, we use a stump." He turned to her with a smile. "You know that big maple stump by the side of the cabin?"

"Yes," she said, puzzled.

"Pa and I cut it off as smooth as we could. Next, he worked at chipping, carving, and even burning it to cut a hollow bowl into the center of it. Then we rigged a spring pole with a wooden pounder attached. I sit up on that stump and pound the kernels in the bowl until they're fine enough for johnnycake."

"It sounds like a lot of work," Emily said.

"I didn't mind that as much as not being able to finish my cabin. I'll work on it evenings when we're through in the fields."

"What fields?" Emily remembered seeing only trees and a few stumps.

"Last year we planted corn in Sally's field. We cleared about an acre of ours and put in my trees and some beans and other vegetables." He flicked the reins over the oxen to keep them moving through the soft spots in the snow. "We've continued to cut trees for wood to clear more land. We need to grow a lot more to feed the growing family."

"And you'll need more land for your trees," she said softly.

He smiled at her. "I'm going to build that orchard. You'll be baking apple pies in a few years."

If I'm still here, she murmured to herself.

"I'll work on my cabin to make it a house. I can't ask a woman to marry me if I don't have a home for her."

Emily couldn't speak. Did he just ask me to marry him? *No,* she told herself, *he said he had to finish the cabin before he could ask.*

"I'll do whatever I can to help you," Emily offered.

"I like that idea. We'll work together."

They arrived at the sugar camp. "I'll get the pots we used to boil the sap. We didn't bring them in until we were sure they had completely cooled."

"Do these buckets and augurs go too?" Emily pointed to buckets half hidden behind the woodpile.

"We must have missed those. You have a good eye, Emily. We might have lost them."

They worked side by side putting the camp in order and packing all the equipment that had been left behind.

"I brought some corn bread and cold venison." Emily unwrapped a bag and offered him some food before they started back to the cabin.

"That sounds good. I'm hungry." Jonathan reached over and broke off a piece of the bread.

Along the way back, the snow had softened more in spots until the oxen struggled to keep the runners going. "If this weather keeps up we'd better put the wheels on this sled. When we go to the fort to trade, we'll need it as a wagon. Last year we pulled things with the Indian cart."

"Your father explained how that works." She laughed. "Tommy offered to teach me how to hook it up so Beth and I can go visiting."

"You'll need it to go to the fellowship. Some of those meetings are as far as ten miles away."

"Can you make a round trip in one day?" Emily couldn't imagine how far ten miles would be.

"We can in the summer when it's light early and darkness comes late." He smiled as they pulled up next to the Miller cabin. "During those days we work from dawn to dark to get everything done."

When Emily entered the cabin, she saw Mr. Miller sitting alone on a bench with a mug of tea.

"Where's Tommy?" she asked, glancing around the room.

"His mother missed him, so I told him he needed to stay and take care of her."

"He's a nice little boy." Emily smiled.

Mr. Miller put his mug down. "It's almost as if I have my own boys as little ones again."

"Sally is nice too," she added.

Mr. Miller raised his eyebrows. "You noticed that, did you?"

David had gone out to help his brother put the equipment away and unhook the oxen.

Beth turned from the fire where she had started supper and frowned at her sister. "Emmy, you're too forward."

"I don't mind who knows I care for Sally," Mr. Miller interjected. "I guess you know we plan to marry when the preacher comes."

Emily and Beth looked at each other over his head and smiled. "We'd heard something like that," Emily said.

"David said he'd go over to Colosse soon to see if any mail has come through for us," Beth said. "Maybe he can find out then just when the preacher is due in these parts."

Emily shivered. *I hope there is no message for me.*

eight

David made a trip to Colosse as soon as the weather permitted and returned with news of the circuit preacher's schedule that allowed Mr. Miller and Sally to officially declare their wedding plans. But waiting in Colosse was a letter for Emily.

She stepped outside, away from the happy gathering in the cabin, and walked over to the stump mill. There she stood, with her shawl pulled tight around her arms and shoulders. *I will not cry,* she told herself. *I must not spoil Sally's joy.*

"How bad is it?"

Jonathan's voice startled her. Emily turned to see him close behind her. Tears pressed against her eyelids. "Mother is ordering me to come home."

"She couldn't have received the letter you sent with Phineas," Jonathan said.

"She wrote this one two weeks after we left. We weren't even here yet, and she wanted me to come back." The tears pushed out from the corners of her eyes.

She wanted nothing more than to lay her head on Jonathan's chest. *That would not be proper,* she heard her mother's voice in her mind.

Jonathan seemed to read her thoughts. He stepped forward and pulled her into his arms. She lay her head on his chest and let the sobs wrack her body.

"What will you do?" he asked.

Emily stepped away, her back rigid. "I will not go back," she declared, wiping her cheeks on the corner of her shawl. "She wants me there to marry Henry Richards."

Jonathan looked shocked. "You are promised?"

"No!" Emily said defiantly. "It is simply my mother's desire, but I will not marry that man. He is ugly inside and out."

"Emily, you can't go against your parents' wishes."

"I know the commandments of God, but even God wouldn't expect me to marry that horrid man."

Jonathan stepped back and looked at her. "If you're promised, then I cannot speak with your father."

Emily looked up at him. *Did he say he wanted to speak with my father? But why? Does he mean—?*

"Jonathan, why do you want to speak with my father?" she asked, her voice trembling.

He tilted his head as he gazed down on her upturned face. "I thought you knew, Emily. I want to ask him for your hand. I want you to be my wife."

"Oh!" Her heart pounded in her ears.

"And I cannot ask him until I can offer you a home."

"Oh!" she said again. She took a deep breath. "We can build that cabin together. Then you can write to my father."

Jonathan still looked worried. "What about your mother? What will you do now?"

"I will do nothing for now. She'll get the letter I sent with Phineas, and that will give us more time. And even if I have to make a trip back to Connecticut to talk to my father, he won't make me marry someone I don't love."

Jonathan pulled her to him again. "We'll pray for God to guide us. I love you and want you to be with me always," he whispered.

Emily rested against him for a moment. In spite of her mother's letter, she felt a glow of happiness. *Jonathan loves me and wants to marry me!*

She stepped out of the shelter of his arms. "I have prayed every day, since I saw you ride out of Ashford, that someday we would be together. God has allowed me to be here, and if it's His will, I feel sure He'll show us a way to marry and make our home here." She smiled and added, "And grow lots of apples."

"Shall we tell the others?"

"No, this day belongs to Sally and your father. The preacher will be here sometime in May, and we'll have a wedding for them. Next time it will be for us," she said, with a confidence she did not feel.

Jonathan held her arm as he guided her back to the cabin. "In God's time it will happen."

❧

April brought days of bright warm sun that melted the snow. It also brought cold days of wind and rain. The path to Sally's became a sea of mud. Jonathan laid bark to make a path to the barn.

"I'll go over to my cabin to work," Jonathan announced to his father and David one morning.

"What can you do?" his father asked.

"I can start laying the hemlock bark for a roof. I got as far as putting up the poles for a roof base last fall. Once I have the roof on I can start on a floor inside."

"Do you have any basswood split?" his father asked.

"No, I got too busy grinding corn last fall." Jonathan sighed. "But there's some growing nearby."

"I'll come with you and start cutting the basswood and smoothing out some floor boards," his father said. "We can't start any work in the fields until the ground thaws and the weather gets warm."

"What can I do?" Emily asked quietly.

"Did you make mud pies as a child?"

Emily thought Mr. Miller was teasing her. "Yes, and I didn't burn them."

"David can dig you some clay from the creek bank, and you can chink the spaces between the logs. It'll keep the wind out when winter comes."

"Is there anything I should do?" Beth asked.

"You can take care of Phillip and have a meal ready when we come in this evening," David told his wife, smiling and giving her a hug.

Emily looked into Jonathan's eyes, which seemed bright with hope. *We will get this cabin built soon.* Excitement filled her. *Maybe we can be married by fall.*

"We'll cut down that basswood first," Jonathan told his father. "I need the basswood bark to tie the hemlock on the roof beams."

"Come on, Emily," David said. "It sounds as if you and I are going to play in the mud today." He turned to his wife, chuckling. "Someday you'll complain when Phillip comes in covered with mud, and I'll remind you of how to build a cabin."

The three men and Emily started out. Passing the open field on the way to Jonathan's cabin, Emily suddenly cried out. "Look! The apple trees are starting to bud!"

At once, Jonathan crossed the path to look closer. "You're right! It seems as if all of them lived except one. I'll plant the seeds I started at my place."

"You mean Beth and I get the first apples?" David asked.

Jonathan waved his arms in an arc over the field. "Someday this land between us will be filled with apple trees."

"You have big dreams," his brother teased.

❧

Work on the cabin proceeded with the three men working together. Emily even learned to pull the buckets of clay with the Indian cart. To reach the logs, she had to climb a ladder carrying a bucket of clay. Coming back down for another load, she turned in surprise when Jonathan took the empty bucket out of her hand.

"You need a rest," he told her. "I'll get you a drink of cold water."

Emily felt as if every bone in her small body ached, but she would never complain. Jonathan might send her back to the cabin, and she longed to be near him.

When he handed her the dipper of water, he started to laugh. "Did you get any clay on the logs?"

She felt him flick a patch of muck off her face, then gently rub the spot where it had been. Looking down, Emily saw splotches of gray on her bodice. The hem of her skirt dragged with the weight of the clay she had soaked up while digging in the creek bed. She couldn't hold back the giggle that escaped when she thought how she must look.

"You'll have your cabin soon," Jonathan whispered.

Emily's heart beat faster at his promise.

As the weather improved, the men spent more time preparing the fields. They cut the trees to clear more land, but the wet ground and rains meant they would have to burn the stumps later in the season.

"We'll take the ashes to the commercial asheries later this summer," Jonathan told Emily and Beth one day.

"Can you bring us back soap when you do?" Beth asked. "We'll need more by then."

"If we had some lye, we could make our own soap," Emily said.

"I also plan to bring back glass. That way we can put a window in each cabin. We can open the shutters and gain light without the cold wind."

"We should get some potash kettles so we can boil ashes and make lye. Then you women can make your own soap," David said.

"Always the merchant wanting to find a product to sell," his brother teased.

"Why not? The land is good, and more people will come, so we can have a mercantile waiting to serve them," David retorted.

"And sell soap," Beth added.

"Could we build Jonathan's cabin first?" Emily asked.

"And grow a bigger orchard," Jonathan added.

"I was just sharing my dream," David told them, smiling.

❧

An ox was hitched to a clumsy wooden plow with a v-shaped

harrow. Once the earth was turned over, one of the men followed to throw the seed by hand. David and Jonathan had made a trip to Whitestown to buy seed potatoes.

"If you'll handle the plow, I'll put in the seed corn," Mr. Miller told his older son. "We'll get that field of Sally's in corn like we did last year."

"We should get the potatoes planted as well," Jonathan said. "I don't have all the stumps burned, but we could plant potatoes where I've cut wood for the cabin."

"If you'll do the plowing I'll plant the potatoes," Emily told him.

"What can I do?" Beth asked.

Emily looked at her sister's pale face. Beth never complained. She hadn't even told David she was expecting another child. But Emily knew the baby Beth carried now gave her a lot more trouble than Phillip had.

"I'll show you how to cut the seed potatoes so they're ready for planting," David said. "You know you can't go into the fields and leave Phillip. That will be your way of helping."

Later, when the men had gone outside to get the plows ready for the morning work, Beth stood up from the hearth and put a hand to her back. "I don't seem to have any strength," she murmured.

Emily put a comforting arm around her sister. "It's no wonder. You're not just sick in the morning—you're sick all day."

"I feel so useless. You're working in the fields and helping build the cabin, and I can barely get around enough to cook a meal."

Emily patted her sister's back. "You take care of the baby. I'll try to help more in the house and with Phillip. Are you going to hold up for the fellowship gathering here on Sunday?"

"Oh, yes. I look forward to having people around. I hope we have a good day. I don't think we can fit thirty people in the cabin, though." Beth glanced around their one-room home.

"If it rains, we'll send the men to the barn. They can put

the horse and oxen out in the rain."

"Emily, you're terrible," she said, squeezing her sister's hand, "but I'd be lost without you."

"Sally will be here to help too." Emily crossed the room to throw a log on the fire. "And she knows the people. Maybe someone will know exactly when the preacher is coming, and we can plan her wedding."

"The dress is ready. Has Tommy ever told?" Beth asked.

"He got so excited when Mr. Miller came back that I think he forgot all about it. Oh, Mr. Miller says he's taking Tommy fishing on Saturday so we'll have fresh fish to fry for Sunday."

"That's good, but I'm worried that we won't have enough plates for everyone."

"Jonathan said the families bring their own. Out here they have only enough for their own family."

"I'll ask David to have Sally bring her spider so we can have two pans of fish frying at once."

≈

Sunday brought their warmest day yet. "God is smiling on us," Mr. Miller said. He had left the Indian cart and an ox at Sally's cabin, and she and the children had arrived at the Millers' bright and early for the meeting.

"I hope we have enough food for everyone. David told us not to make johnnycake. Is that right, Sally?" Beth looked at the young woman.

"Yes, by this time of year most families don't have much left but some cornmeal so they'll bring plenty of johnny-cake." She looked in the bucket sitting by the cabin door. "It looks as if Mr. Miller and Tommy caught a good mess of trout. That will be a real treat."

"The Wheelers are coming up the path!" Jonathan called out to the women in the cabin.

More people arrived. Emily and Beth tried to store names to memory. "I'll never remember which children belong to which family," Emily moaned to her sister.

The group gathered outside. The men brought out benches and set up cut logs for more seats. At first, they spent time catching up about the winter months. Then George Miller took out his Bible. Others did the same. Time passed quickly while they read and discussed the Scriptures. Emily felt as if she learned a lot listening to these God-fearing people who braved the elements to start a new life.

I'm proud to be with them. I pray God will show me a way to stay here.

Just then, Sally nodded to her. They slipped into the cabin and started frying fish. When the other women smelled the food cooking, they carried the food they had brought into the cabin.

One of the Wheeler boys looked at the pans piled high with johnnycake and turned to his brothers. "You'd better get Harriet to sing for us."

Emily took a pan of fried fish outside to put on the table then and was shocked to see some older boys bullying a young girl of about twelve. "What are you doing?" she asked them sternly.

"Don't mind Harriet, Miss Emily. It takes some coaxing to get her to sing for her dinner."

"Oh!" she exclaimed and turned to the girl. "Are you going to sing?"

People gathered around the girl, with most grinning widely. Emily realized they had heard it before.

Then Harriet stood up, folded her hands in front of her and sang:

> If you to Scriba draw nigh,
> You to our fashion must comply,
> All you who would your fortune make
> Must learn the use of johnnycake.
>
> It serves for food all through the day

First in the morning here they say,
"Come, burn a crust and coffee make
And save our tea by johnnycake."

For dinner they will take a slice;
They eat it, thinking it is so nice.
Then for luncheon too they take
Another piece of johnnycake.

When the supper table it is spread
They smack their lips and nod their heads,
And a good supper they partake
Of nothing but a johnnycake.

I'd have you use this homemade song,
All you whose stomachs are not strong;
The richest man in all the state
May yet be glad of johnnycake.

Harriet went back to her mother as people clapped and cheered for her.

"It wasn't quite a hymn for Sunday," Mrs. Wheeler said by way of apology, but she still glowed with pride in her daughter.

"She just sang the truth," Rufus Wheeler said in defense of his sister. "Without johnnycake, we would all be hungry some days."

"I guess we should be thankful for what the Lord gives us," Mr. Miller agreed. "Now let's bless this food, johnnycake and all."

nine

While the women were clearing away the dishes and washing up, Emily spoke quietly with Mrs. Wheeler. "Sally says you are the nurse around here."

"I do what I can," the older lady said. "Colonel Dewey's wife knows the herbs and their uses, but she doesn't speak our language."

"I'm worried about my sister. She's having another baby."

Mrs. Wheeler patted Emily's arm. "It's natural enough, Dear. She should be fine."

"She was when Phillip was born, but this time she's sick all the time. She eats almost nothing and has no strength. Is there something I can do for her?"

Mrs. Wheeler looked over at Beth who sat on a bench with Phillip in her arms. "She does look somewhat peaked. How far along is she?"

Emily blushed. "I'm not sure. Less than three months, I think."

"From what I've seen, if the baby isn't right, the good Lord takes them. You should be ready if your sister has a miscarriage."

Emily felt a knot of fear turn in her stomach. "I don't have any idea what to do."

"Have some old cloths ready—she'll need them. Then try to keep her resting for a few days to get her strength back. That boy of hers is heavy for her to be lifting while she's in the family way."

"I've been trying to help in the fields, but I'll stay home and take care of Phillip. Maybe Beth will rest more if I'm there to do the cooking and washing," Emily said, as much to herself as to Mrs. Wheeler.

"You're a good girl, Emily. How soon before we plan your wedding?"

Emily felt her face flush. "Jonathan has to finish his cabin first, then he said he will ask my father for my hand."

Mrs. Wheeler raised her eyebrows. "It isn't usually that formal out here."

"My mother doesn't want me to stay here," Emily admitted.

"It shouldn't be up to your mother, although that's important, of course. It should be up to God. We'll pray for your happiness."

If I could just get word of Father's blessing. . .

Mrs. Wheeler turned to leave. "You send for me if you need help with your sister."

"Thank you. It helps to know I can talk with another woman." But Emily did not feel relieved as she glanced across the room at her sister.

❧

Beth spent more and more time lying down. She thought it might help her carry the baby better. Even David was becoming concerned.

One day the men went early to work in the fields. Emily was standing in the yard over the washtub when she heard Beth cry out. She ran into the cabin and knelt beside the bed where her sister was lying.

"Beth, what is it?"

"The pain is as bad as when Phillip was born," she said weakly.

"What can I do to help you?"

"Pray," Beth said, a faint smile on her pale lips. "It is up to God now."

Emily knew all things were up to God, but she wondered about His timing. Lovingly, she tended to Beth, offering her sips of cool water and a cold cloth for her face. The pain grew more intense, and Emily found that all she could do was pray for it to end.

After several hours had passed, Beth drew a ragged breath. "It's over, Emmy. My little one will never see this earth."

"You'll hold your baby in heaven someday." Emily whispered, wiping her sister's forehead with a wet cloth. "Do you want me to get David now?"

She shook her head. "No, I'm so tired I just want to sleep. Is Phillip all right?"

"He's still napping. I'll take care of him," she assured her.

She brought a basin of fresh water and bathed her sister. Carefully, she folded the salt sack towels under her and covered her with a clean quilt.

"Thank God you are here, Emmy. I don't know what I would do without you." Beth reached out to touch her sister's hand.

Emily kissed her sister before taking the soiled quilt out to the washtub in the yard. She laid the cloths by the door while she fetched a shovel. After digging a grave under one of the apple trees, she prayerfully buried the child that never grew.

I'll write Mother and tell her how sick Beth is. Then she'll understand why I'm not coming home, she thought as she washed the clothes she had left soaking in the tub. *I think I'll write a separate letter to Father. I don't want him to worry about Beth, but both he and Mother must know she needs me now.*

She hung the wet clothes over a piece of rope Jonathan had strung up. *In this heat things will dry quickly.*

⁂

A week later, Sally stopped by the cabin. "Rufus Wheeler came by my place yesterday to say the preacher was staying with them. I told him George and I would come over to make plans for our wedding."

She put Abbie on the floor and watched as the toddler made her way to Phillip, who tried to crawl away from her. But soon the two were playing happily together.

"I think she has missed her playmate," Sally said. "Where is Beth?"

Emily sighed deeply. "She lost the baby last week. She sleeps a lot."

"Oh, Emily, I'm so sorry to hear that. She didn't look well the last time I saw her, so perhaps sleeping is the best thing for her now."

"Now she's afraid she won't have any more children," Emily confided.

"Why don't we have Polly come and talk with her? She can tell her more about how these things happen. When George and I go over to the Wheelers' to talk to the preacher, I'll ask Polly to come and try to cheer Beth up."

"Thank you, Sally. That would mean a great deal. It's been very hard for her, for all of us. But tell me—when do you think you'll get married?"

"Soon, I hope! If George doesn't join our family soon, I think Tommy will run away and come to live here."

Emily laughed. "He does love his 'papa.'" Turning serious, she asked, "Are you sure you want this for yourself, or are you getting married only to make Tommy happy?"

Sally blushed. "I really care for George. It isn't like being young and in love with my Tom. George and I are good friends and will be companions for many years."

Impulsively, Emily hugged her friend. "I pray that you are."

"Who are you talking to, Emmy?" Beth called from her bed.

"Sally is here. Why don't you get up, and we'll have tea?"

Beth came to the table and sat with her sister and Sally while they talked about the upcoming wedding.

"Polly wants us to come to their place," Sally said. "Did she know you were sick, Beth? I wondered why she insisted we come there instead of getting married here."

Emily looked at her sister. "I talked to her," she admitted. "I didn't know how to help you, Beth. She could see you weren't doing well."

"I'll get my strength back soon. Still I'm glad you're going to the Wheelers'. I don't think I'll be up to another fellowship here for a few weeks."

Emily glanced around the room. "Where's Tommy?"

Sally laughed. "You need to ask? He's with George in the vegetable garden."

"I need him. You two enjoy your tea while I round up my helper."

Emily ran across the field and called to Tommy. "Come here a moment. I need to talk to you."

"What is it?" Mr. Miller asked, following the boy.

"Tommy and I have a surprise, so I have to ask you to go back to hoeing weeds," Emily told him as she took the boy's hand.

Mr. Miller raised his eyebrows. "Will you ask Sally to wait till I come in later?"

"She needs to talk to you about plans for the wedding so I'm sure she'll wait. Now Tommy and I have business." Emily and the boy started back to the cabin.

"I didn't tell," Tommy said, shaking his head.

"I know you didn't, but don't you think it's time to tell your mother what we have for her?"

Beth and Sally were still sitting at the table when Tommy and Emily entered the cabin.

"What do you think, Beth? Is it time for Tommy to share our secret with his mother?" Emily asked cheerfully.

Beth nodded, and the smile on her face erased the lines of fatigue.

Emily closed her eyes for a moment and said a quick prayer of thanks when she saw her sister's face brighten. "Come on, Tommy. I have it in my trunk."

Within moments, the boy walked back to his mother with the dress folded across his arms, his face a wreath of smiles.

"What is this?" Sally looked puzzled.

"Miss Emily and Miss Beth made this for you," Tommy

said solemnly, laying the dress in his mother's lap.

"Oh, the blue flowers!" Sally exclaimed as she stood up and held the dress to her. She looked from one sister to the other. "You used your beautiful calico for me?"

"It's your wedding dress, Mommy," Tommy crowed.

"It certainly is," Sally said with tears slipping down her cheeks.

The wedding was set for the following Sunday. Beth insisted she would be well enough to go, and David told her he would take her in the cart.

"What will we take, Emmy?" Beth asked, standing up to help clear the table.

"I thought I would use some of our wheat flour and bake sourdough biscuits. We don't have butter, but we could take syrup to pour on them."

"Poor Harriet won't get to sing her song," Beth said, laughing.

The sound echoed in the cabin and brought smiles to everyone there. Beth would be all right.

※

Sunday dawned bright and clear. Everyone had gathered at the Wheelers' for their usual fellowship meeting, but this week they were celebrating a wedding.

Sally looked radiant in her new dress. George Miller's pride shone as he stood next to his bride. He held Abbie in his arms, and Tommy stood at his mother's side, while the couple pledged their vows before God and their friends.

Harriet Wheeler had gathered a bouquet of trilliums from the woods to decorate the food table. The wedding made the Fellowship's time together all the more special.

David and Jonathan cheered their father and his new bride as they left for their own home, and Beth joined in the celebration. Emily silently thanked God to see her sister looking like herself again.

Beth continued to regain her strength, but Emily worked

around the cabin daily to watch over both her sister and her nephew. At times, she wondered about Jonathan's progress on his cabin. *The men have so much work cutting wood and taking care of the fields that he surely can't have much time to spend on it.*

"Beth, why don't you take a nap, and Phillip and I will go outside and get some air?"

"Emmy, you can't carry that child all the way to Jonathan's," she said, with a twinkle in her eyes.

"I can put him on my shoulders," she said, wondering how her sister knew what she was planning.

The boy was heavy, but Emily carried him the mile to the new cabin where she found Jonathan digging in the earth.

"Hello!" he greeted. "I can see I need to make a cart for Phillip. He's too big for you to carry. Set him down and rest."

"I would, but he'll crawl in the dirt."

Jonathan laughed. "He's a boy and will love getting dirty."

"What are you digging? I thought you already had a well." Emily looked into the hole.

"I do. Here, I'll draw a bucket of cold water. I'm thirsty, and you must be too, after carrying Phillip all that way." He pointed to an upturned log for her to sit on.

Emily watched Phillip as he crawled a little way and sat down to run his fingers through the dirt.

Jonathan handed her a dipper of water. "See, I knew he would like playing out here."

"You didn't tell me what you're digging."

"It's a root cellar. We need a cool place, but one that doesn't freeze, for storing potatoes and other fruits and vegetables— like the one David and Beth have."

Emily felt a glow of pleasure when he talked as if the cabin were theirs together.

"Come look inside. I've put up some shelves for dishes."

Emily noticed that Phillip was occupied by the dirt pile at the side of the cabin.

"The shelves look lovely," she said, admiring his work. "Where are your dishes? We could put them up now."

Jonathan smiled. "I don't have any, but I thought perhaps a certain young lady might have some that we could put on the shelves."

"Oh!" she said, her face heating. "But I don't have any either."

"Well, I guess we'll need to get some for you then," he said softly.

"Perhaps I could start a rag rug to go in front of the fireplace," she said, walking around the empty cabin.

Suddenly she thought of the baby. "I'd better check on Phillip," she said, hurrying out the door. She ran back at once.

"He's gone!" she cried. "Jonathan, he's gone!"

"He can't have gone far. He doesn't crawl that fast," Jonathan said. "I'll check around the cabin on that side. You go the other way, and we'll find the little rascal."

He'll think I am not fit to raise children, Emily worried. *Where could Phillip have gotten to so quick?*

Seeing the pile of dirt next to where Jonathan had been working, she thought the baby might have crawled behind it. Walking toward the spot, she saw the shovel stuck in the ground where Jonathan had left it. She continued until she stood next to the hole. Something caught her eye.

Emily screamed.

"What is it? What's wrong?" Jonathan ran to her side.

Emily stood with one hand over her mouth and the other pointing into the hole.

Phillip lay still at the bottom of the root cellar.

ten

"First Beth loses her baby, and now I've killed her son," Emily cried, the tears rolling down her cheeks.

She watched as Jonathan grabbed the ladder, climbed down into the hole and carefully picked up the small body. Cradling the child in one arm, he climbed back up.

"He's breathing."

"Oh, what have I done?" she cried, reaching out to touch her nephew gently.

"We need to find out where he's hurt. Try moving his arms and legs to see if they're broken," Jonathan instructed.

Phillip started to squirm, then yelled. They knew nothing was broken when he waved his arms about and kicked his legs.

"He's only had the wind knocked out of him," Jonathan concluded, smiling. "He'll be fine."

Emily felt suddenly weak and sat down on the ground.

"Are you all right?" Jonathan asked, kneeling beside her with the crying infant in his arms. "Are you going to faint?"

"I have never fainted in my life. I just wanted to catch my breath and thank God for protecting Phillip." She reached for her nephew.

Jonathan laughed as Phillip struggled to get free of her arms. "I think he wants to get back to the dirt."

Emily couldn't hold the squirming boy and watched while he crawled back to the dirt pile. "If my mother knew what I've done, she would order me home tomorrow."

Jonathan sat on the ground next to her. "We won't tell her. And if you like, we won't even tell Beth."

"I should never have let him out of my sight."

"Children get into trouble all the time. You can't be with them every minute. Didn't you have accidents when you were growing up?"

"Once I fell out of a tree. I never told Mother about that."

"Did you tell your sister?"

Emily nodded. "She cleaned me up before Mother saw me."

Jonathan reached out to take Emily's hand. "And don't you think she'll forgive you now? You didn't mean any harm."

"I can't ask her not to write Mother." Emily watched Phillip tossing dirt into the air. "But I don't think she will."

Emily stood to her feet reluctantly. She did not want to leave Jonathan. "I'd better take Phillip home before something else happens."

"I'll go with you." Jonathan picked up the little boy. Tired and covered with dirt from the day's adventures, the child fell asleep at once on his shoulder.

As Emily looked at them, a lump rose in her throat. *What will our children be like?* she wondered. *Dear Lord, please let Jonathan and me have lots of children. And please let my father send his blessing soon.* With his cabin well on its way to being finished, Jonathan had written a letter to her father a few weeks earlier.

Beth was sitting in the sun by the door of the cabin when they returned. "What happened to my little boy?" She looked at his grimy face and laughed.

"Oh, Beth, I took my eyes off him for a minute, and he fell into a hole!" Emily confessed.

Beth held her son up over her head and smiled at his sleepy giggle. "He doesn't seem to have been hurt as much as you. Accidents happen. Don't you remember falling out of a tree?"

"Yes, I do."

"Is there any other mischief I should know about?" Jonathan asked, with a twinkle in his eyes.

"Well, of course all children get into trouble. It did seem as if Emmy got into more than I did, but I guess that's what I want to remember." Beth laughed. "At least I should be experienced then with my own children." She carried Phillip to the cabin. "Come on, little man—it's time to clean you up."

❧

The summer grew hot. The men were up before dawn and often didn't get back until dark. Smoke filled the air from the stumps they burned. They collected ashes and kept the crops weeded.

Emily fretted at the slow progress on completing the final details of Jonathan's cabin, but she knew all the other chores had to be done first. Meanwhile, neighbors helped George and Sally Miller add a room to their cabin.

"Now I have room for my loom," Sally said with joy one day as the women worked together in the shade near the cabin. "I can't weave pretty calico, but we'll have lots of homespun. I planted a quart of flaxseed, and it's growing well. We'll even have linen."

"What we need are some sheep," Beth said, raveling a sock with a big hole and winding the yarn to be reknitted. "My spinning wheel is still in the loft."

Emily worked on the rag rug to go in front of the fireplace in Jonathan's cabin. "Now that you have a bigger cabin," she said to Sally, "I think the men plan to build a new barn to hold more animals. Perhaps we could suggest one or two sheep."

"Will Jonathan be living at his place soon? Maybe they'll build the barn there," Sally said.

Emily kept her head down so the others couldn't read her expression. *I pray we hear before winter.* She reminded herself that it would take weeks for the letter to reach Ashford and more weeks after that for an answer to come back. She sighed deeply.

Beth looked at her. "We'll have to wait and see."

"Why don't we go swimming?" Sally suggested.

"It's so hot, but do you think we dare?" Beth asked.

"Who's going to stop us?" Sally said, her eyes sparkling as she laid down her sewing.

"I know a good spot! It's where we dig clay to chink the logs," Emily said. "It's between here and Jonathan's. We can walk it with the children."

"Tommy and George have gone fishing," Sally said. "George fished so much of his life that he can't seem to give it up."

"I'm glad. The fresh fish are a welcome treat," Emily said.

"He bartered for a small boat, so he and Tommy can go out on the lake."

"Oh, is that safe?" Beth asked, an anxious tone in her voice.

Sally shrugged. "Well, he fished the Atlantic Ocean for years. I guess he can manage Lake Ontario."

"I've got some soap left. I'll get it and some salt sacks." Emily carried her partially made rug back into the cabin.

With Abbie and Phillip in the small cart Jonathan had made, the three women set off to follow the creek.

"See—it's deep enough to get wet all over," Emily said, pointing to the pool.

"Are you going in?" Beth asked, her eyes round with wonder.

"Yes, I am." Emily pulled off her shoes and stockings.

"Me too," Sally chimed in. "You go first, Emily, and I'll watch the children." She pointed to the two little ones who were sitting at the water's edge, splashing, laughing, and having a grand time.

Beth removed her shoes and stockings too and holding up her skirt waded into the water. "Oh, it feels so good." She turned to look at her sister. "Emily, what are you doing?"

She pulled her dress over her head and ran into the water. With just her head above the water, she called back, "This is like heaven! Will you hand me the soap, Beth?"

Her sister waded out with the soap in her hand. "You weren't wearing a petticoat."

"It's too hot for all those clothes. I'll have to go home without a shift too. This one is all wet." Before Beth could scold more, Emily ducked her head under the water. "You girls need to try this!" she called from the center of the pool where she was sudsing her hair. "It's a lot better than a wash basin bath."

"Go ahead, Beth. I'll stay with the children. When Emily comes out I'll take a turn," Sally said.

"It does look cool and clean." Beth unbuttoned her bodice and walked back to dry land to lay her clothes on a bush.

By now the children were soaking wet. Their mothers stripped their wet clothes off and bathed them amid squeals and laughter. Emily took the children's wet things and laid them on a sunny rock to dry. She sat in her shift letting the breeze blow over her cool body.

Beth sat down next to her sister. "You had a good idea."

"It wasn't my idea. Sally suggested we go swimming. Turn around, Beth, and I'll comb out your hair."

"It feels so good to be clean all over." Her sister sighed in contentment.

Sally joined them. Her red-gold curls shone as bright as new copper.

"Why don't you sit in the sun?" Emily asked.

Sally laughed. "I already have the face of a thousand freckles. I don't need any more."

"How long have we been here? We need to get back to start supper," Beth said as she wound her hair back into a bun.

"I hope George is back with fish," Sally added. "Oh, this is still wet," she said, tucking her hair into her sunbonnet.

"I'm going to let mine stay loose so it will dry," Emily declared.

She took Phillip out of the water and dried him quickly with a salt sack. Then she started putting his clothes on amidst howls of protest.

Suddenly the bushes parted, and Jonathan stood there. "What are you doing to that child?" he asked, pretending to scowl. Then he smiled. "I was on my way to the cabin and heard the ruckus. I came to see if you needed help."

"I wouldn't be surprised if you came to take a swim and found us here already," Sally said, laughing.

Jonathan was silent. He gazed at Emily as she struggled with Phillip. *She looks so tiny.* He noticed the sun playing with the ripples in her chestnut-colored curls. *I've never seen her hair loose.* His heart skipped a beat. *I see her on her mattress by the fire, but she always has her hair in a braid.* He sighed deeply. He longed to have her by his side as his wife.

Phillip kept crying until Beth reached out for him. "Let me take him. He'll fall asleep in the cart going back."

Emily gave the boy to his mother and turned toward Jonathan. She stood there for a moment, caught in his gaze. He stepped closer to her.

"You're beautiful," he murmured.

Emily said nothing. The look in her eyes told him she loved him.

"Come on, Emmy. We'll be on our way and let the gentleman have a cooling swim," Sally said.

Jonathan watched as Emily turned away from him and hurried after her sister and Sally.

❧

"Look what we caught, Mama!" Tommy called when he saw his mother approaching the cabin. "Papa says he'll cook them over a fire outside so you don't have to heat up the cabin."

"I like that idea," Sally said, looking at the fish and greeting her husband. "Will we cook them here to share with everyone?"

"That was my idea if you agree," he told her. "Your hair looks beautiful down your back," he said quietly to her when she pulled off her bonnet.

She smiled at him. "We've been swimming, and it got wet. I need to comb it out now and braid it." Then she turned to Emily. "Would you like me to braid your hair after I do mine?"

"I need to put on some dry clothes," Emily said. "Then I would love for you to fix my hair."

Just then Beth came back into the room after settling the sleeping little ones on her bed. "What do I need to do to get the fish ready?"

"You relax, and Tommy and I will cook tonight," her father-in-law told her.

"Like Colonel Dewey told us?" the boy asked.

Mr. Miller nodded his head. "You bring a few slabs of bark over here while I get a fire going. We'll have a feast for David and Jonathan when they come home," he told the boy.

Emily was dressed in dry clothes with her hair braided when Jonathan walked into the yard. She felt her face burn when she saw the tender look on his face.

"I liked you better the way you looked at the creek," he said softly.

eleven

The oppressive heat bore down on the settlers. The men came in exhausted at night. The women tried to cook over an open fire outside to keep the cabin as cool as possible.

One night, Jonathan climbed the ladder to his bed in the loft. He came back within minutes, carrying a quilt over his shoulder. "You could bake bread up there. I'm sleeping outside."

Phillip was fussing and couldn't sleep. Beth discovered he had a heat rash but was unsuccessful in quieting the child.

"Let me take him," David said. "We'll sleep outside with Jonathan. Why don't you girls fix a bed by the door? Some cool air will be coming in from there, and the shutters are open on the other side. If there's a breeze, you'll feel it."

Emily wiped the sweat off her forehead. "That sounds good to me."

Once the men had moved outside, Emily pulled her mattress over to the door. "I'm not going to use a quilt," she said. "The men are gone, and it may be a little cooler."

The women slept restlessly. Emily didn't know how long it had been when she heard the first faint rumbles. She lay still, not wanting to wake her sister.

But just then Beth sat up with a start. "Did you hear that?"

Before Emily could answer, a flash of lightning brightened the sky. "We'd better wake up the men."

"Oh, I'm sure they'll hear the thunder and get in ahead of the rain."

David appeared in the doorway with Phillip still asleep in his arms.

Beth jumped up to take her son and put him back in the box he had used as a bed. Emily pulled her mattress back

81

from the door and wrapped a shawl around her nightgown-clad shoulders.

The lightning and thunder grew closer, and Jonathan stepped inside the cabin, tossing his quilt over a bench. "I checked on the stock, and they're restless but all right. I felt the first drops of rain."

"The vegetables in the garden were wilted. This is a blessing." Beth stood in the door next to David, looking out at the storm.

Jonathan sat down on the bench and motioned for Emily to join him. Pulling the shawl tighter around her, she eased down next to him.

"Do you always braid your hair at night?"

"Yes."

"Maybe someday I can coax you to change that habit."

Emily felt her face burn. A crash of thunder saved her from having to answer.

The rain pelted the roof.

"It's a regular cloudburst," David said from the door.

"The cool air is wonderful," Beth declared. "We'll be able to get some sleep now."

Emily could see Jonathan's face in the flashes of lightning. He seemed to glow with emotion. She longed to nestle within the circle of his strong arms but knew she must not. "I'd better move my bed back into the corner," she murmured, standing up quickly and walking away from the bench.

The rain continued to fall gently after the storm moved on. When Emily woke the next morning, the sun was shining brightly.

"Oh, I overslept," she muttered, jumping up.

She could see that David had left, so she hurried to the back of the cabin where the corner was curtained off and changed into her dress. Stepping outside the cabin she could smell coffee.

"Good morning," Jonathan greeted her when she peered out

the door. "It took awhile, but I got a fire going and put on some coffee. There's hot water if you want to make more mush."

"I'm sorry I'm so late."

"We all got a good rest after the cooling rain. I kept the fire outside—the cool won't last."

Jonathan's prediction proved right. The rain left the garden watered, helping things grow, but the heat of summer returned.

"The berries are ripe in the meadow," Mr. Miller told the women when he and Tommy stopped by to give them some fresh fish.

"I'll pick some berries to dry for the winter," Emily declared.

"Don't dry them all. I want a fresh berry cobbler," Jonathan said, then turned to his father. "How are you, Pa?"

"We're doing very well, Son," his father said. Then he held up the string of fish he was leaving for Beth to cook. "Maybe we should salt some of these for winter."

"I thought I'd get the smokehouse going and do up a batch or two," Jonathan told him.

While the men talked about fish, the women prepared the dinner.

A day or two later Emily remembered the berries. Phillip had been fussing all morning, and Beth looked worn out. "Let me take Phillip in the cart. He can play while I pick berries and be out of your way for a little while. Maybe you could take a nap."

"I'd better get back to that basket of mending," Beth said. "But it would be nice to have a few quiet hours," she admitted, "if you are sure he won't be a bother."

"Hey, little nephew, how about a ride in the cart?"

Emily was rewarded with a big smile and a chortle of pleasure. "I'll get the cart ready and find a bucket for the berries."

Heading for the meadow, Emily could see the smoke where David and Jonathan were burning stumps. She sang to Phillip as she pulled the tripod pole with the box on the back where he sat. He laughed and pointed at the different things he saw on his bumpy ride.

"No more fussy baby," Emily said quietly as she looked back at him.

When they reached the edge of the meadow, she found a place in the shade by the forest and spread the quilt from the cart. She set Phillip down and played with him until he fell asleep.

"Now I can pick berries," Emily murmured, picking up her bucket. "As long as he sleeps, he won't crawl away."

She started near the sleeping child, plucking off the plump blackberries and dropping them into the bucket. Enjoying the afternoon, her mind naturally wandered to thoughts of Jonathan. *I have a little wheat flour I can mix with the cornmeal and make a big cobbler. He will like that.*

She kept glancing back at Phillip. *I'm getting farther away, but as long as he sleeps he'll be all right,* she reasoned, continuing to follow where the berries were thickest.

She heard a rustling sound and turned, thinking Phillip had awakened. She stood frozen to the ground as a large black bear ambled out of the woods near the sleeping child. Emily tried to scream, but no sound would come from her throat. Dropping the bucket, she ran toward the bear. He showed no signs of having seen her and, walking over to the quilt, sniffed the baby.

Suddenly Emily regained her voice and shouted at the bear, waving her apron.

The bear looked up, stared at the woman for a moment, and slowly turned and lumbered back into the trees. Emily snatched the sleeping child into her arms and ran toward the stream of smoke she could see rising over the tree line.

Jolted awake, Phillip started to cry, but Emily didn't hear him over her pounding heart. She clutched him tightly to her and kept running.

Jonathan heard a loud crashing in the brush and glanced up to see Emily, with the child in her arms and a terrified expression on her face. He dropped the stick he had been using to stir the fire and dashed over to her. Perspiration and tears streamed down her cheeks, bright red as the fire he'd been tending.

David had also heard the commotion and ran across the field. He immediately took his son in his arms and tried to quiet him.

"You take care of the baby, and I'll take care of Emily," Jonathan told his brother. He took Emily by the arm and led her to an unburned tree stump, motioning to her to sit down.

Still gasping for breath, she could barely speak.

"I can't understand you, Emily," he told her gently, still holding her arm. "But you're safe here."

"Bear!" she finally managed to say, waving her hands in the direction from which she had come. "Bear!"

Jonathan looked at the place where she pointed. "There's no bear chasing you now. You're safe."

He picked up a jug of water, pulled out the cork, and tipped it so she could drink some. Then he took the corner of her apron, wet it with the water, and gently wiped her face.

At last, Emily was breathing normally again, and Phillip was resting in his father's arms.

"Can you tell us what happened now?" Jonathan asked.

"I was picking berries in the meadow. Phillip was asleep on a quilt near the woods." She put her hand over her breast as if trying to still her heart. "A bear came out of the woods near Phillip and started sniffing him. At first I was so scared I couldn't yell. Then I waved my apron and screamed till he went back into the woods." She collapsed into Jonathan's arms.

The feel of her in his arms sent waves of protectiveness through him. "I won't let anything hurt you," he murmured against her ear.

"I'd better get them back to the cabin," David said.

"We can't leave the fires unattended."

"It won't take long, and I'll come right back to check on things. You're the best shot. You go after the bear," David said with a smile.

Jonathan stood up, still holding Emily by the arms. As she regained her feet, he held her close for a moment while thanking God for keeping her safe.

"Come, Dearest—I'll take you back to the cabin."

Emily glanced at him and smiled faintly at the word of endearment.

Jonathan kept a protective hold on her arm until they reached the yard of the cabin.

David carried Phillip to his mother and explained what had happened. Phillip laughed when his mother put him on the floor with empty thread spools to play with.

"He slept through the whole thing," David said with a sigh. "The Lord does look after his own."

Jonathan led Emily to a bench and went to fix her a cup of tea.

"I'll do that," Beth said, taking the kettle of water he had brought from the outside fire.

"I'll get back to watch the fires till they burn down more," David said and kissed his wife good-bye.

Jonathan climbed up to the loft for a moment and came down with his rifle. He kneeled at Emily's side with the gun on his arm.

"I'll get your bucket of berries," he said, smiling tenderly into her eyes. "After all, you promised me a cobbler."

"Be careful," she cautioned him, glancing at the gun, then gazing into his eyes.

"You scared that poor bear with your apron. I think I can handle him with a gun." Jonathan laughed and rose to leave the cabin.

Emily took the cup her sister offered her. "I get into more trouble. I'd better not take Phillip out any more."

Beth pointed to the happy child on the floor rolling spools

and crawling after them. "His nap did him good." She sat down next to Emily with her own cup of tea. "And I was grateful for the quiet time."

ꙮ

David returned before dark. "Have you heard any word from Jonathan?"

Emily caught her breath. "No. You don't think the bear got him, do you?"

David laughed. "That bear doesn't have a chance. You picked all his berries so Jonathan will save him from starving." He looked out the unshuttered window. "We have an hour or so before dark. I'll go and see if Jonathan needs help."

The sun had set when Beth and Emily heard the men coming through the yard. Hurrying outside, they saw a large pile of black fur strapped on the cart.

Jonathan dropped the pole and carried a bucket to Emily. With a bow he handed it to her. "I think you dropped this," he said, chuckling.

"You shot the bear!" she exclaimed. Turning to her sister, she asked, "Do you know what to do with a bear?"

"Make a rug?" Beth suggested, frowning.

"We haven't skinned him out yet, but I'm sure you'll make candles," David said.

The women looked at each other, then back to the brothers who were laughing at them. "Candles?"

"This old boy is fat," Jonathan said. "He's full of enough tallow for candles that will last all winter."

"We'll need to ask Sally how to make candles," Emily told her sister. "But right now I'm going to make a cobbler for our hero."

twelve

The men worked by firelight to skin the bear. They piled the slabs of fat to be rendered on a board by the cabin.

"What will we do with all this meat?" Beth asked. "It won't keep long in this heat."

Jonathan stood up, wiping the sweat from his face with the back of his hand. "We have a lot of meat here. It'll probably take two crocks to put it down to cure. I'll ride over to Pa's first thing in the morning and get a big crock. We have one here, so we can cure some hams, and we have lots of sugar to make it a sugar cure. Do you girls have a meat grinder?"

"Yes, we do," Emily told him.

"Good—you can grind up some of this old boy and make sausage," Jonathan said.

"I brought recipes for sausage, and I think we have spice we can use," she told Jonathan. "But how can we smoke it?"

"We'll wrap rolls in salt sacks," Beth said. "Then we can lay it on the racks in the smokehouse."

"What would we do without salt sacks?" Emily giggled.

"You'll be getting some more. After we salt down this hide and make brine for ham, we'll be almost out of salt. David and I will have to make a trip for more."

"When you go to your father's, will you ask Sally to come and show us how to make candles?" Emily asked. "We can share this meat with them too. They're having the fellowship on Sunday, and Sally can cook a pot of bear stew." She turned to go inside. "If you're almost finished with the bear, I'll make some fresh coffee and dish up the cobbler."

"That sounds good to me," Jonathan said, scraping the last bit of hide loose. "We can put this meat in the box by the creek to stay cold tonight. We'll start cutting it up tomorrow."

"You mean I will," his brother teased. "You already volunteered to ride to Pa's."

David cut the carcass into pieces that would fit into the wooden box they had buried in the mud by the creek. The cool water rushing by would keep the meat cold.

"You'd better find another big box and start digging, Jonathan. One box won't hold all this."

The men worked into the night to get the bear stored away. Then they washed in the creek and came in to enjoy the cobbler and fell exhausted into bed.

In the morning, Jonathan stopped long enough to drink the cup of coffee Emily offered him. "The sooner I get on my way, the sooner I can be back here to help."

"Please ask Sally about the candles," Emily reminded him.

"You don't want to be in the dark next winter?" he teased her.

David screwed the meat grinder onto the table and looked at his wife. "Can you work this?"

"I used to grind vegetables for Kate to make soup."

"Meat is going to be a little harder."

"We'll take turns," Emily told him.

By midmorning, when Jonathan returned, the sisters had a pot of meat cooking over the open fire.

"Oh, my arms ache," Emily said, sitting down on a bench with a thump.

"I'll take over for awhile," Beth told her, stuffing some meat into the grinder.

Jonathan laughed at the two of them. "You need some muscle to work that machine. Here—let me do it."

"Gladly," Beth said, sitting down next to her sister. "Let me get the cramps out of my arms, and I'll start mixing the spices and roll this so it's ready for smoking."

"Pa and Sally are on their way over and are bringing the crock." He looked at Emily. "I didn't forget the candles.

Sally said she would bring the molds too."

"I'll pull some carrots and onions out of the garden to go with the meat, and we can have stew for supper," she said. "Do you think they'll spend the night?"

"If they do, I'll sleep outside, and they can have the loft," Jonathan offered.

The ground meat piled up rapidly with him at the grinder.

"You'd better get the salt sacks while I mix the sausage," Beth told her sister.

"How long will it have to smoke?" Emily asked Jonathan. "It'll be nice to have something different to eat."

"It should take a couple of days anyway. As soon as I finish grinding this meat, I'll start the smokehouse fire."

David stuck his head in the door. "I have our crock with a haunch of bear ready for the cure. Do you want me to mix it?"

"Yes," Beth said. "We're making the sausage."

"This is the last sack of salt," David said, carrying the bag from the corner storage spot.

"Maybe we can head out next week," his brother said.

"How far do you have to go? Can you get salt at Fort Ontario?" Beth asked.

"It costs a lot there. Colonel Dewey said they mine salt near Onondaga Lake. I thought we'd take the wagon and go down there," David said.

"How long will you be gone?" his wife asked.

"I'm not sure. It must be about sixty miles, so it'll take us about four days to get there. It might be longer coming back with a heavy load for the oxen to pull," David told her.

By the time they were putting the sausage in the smokehouse, the Millers arrived.

"Are we going to make candles?" Tommy asked glumly.

"Yes," Emily answered, "but why do you look so unhappy?"

"I hate to make wicks," the little boy grumbled.

"Well, I don't know how. Will you teach me?"

Tommy perked up. "Do you have any rags?"

"You mean like my rag rug?" Emily asked.

He nodded his head. "We have to twist pieces of cloth and not let them unwind."

"I'll get my rag bag, and we'll work together."

"I have a candle mold to make six. By the looks of all that tallow, this is going to take days," Sally told them. "We'll have enough for all of us this winter."

Tommy groaned. "I hate to make wicks," he declared again.

"Come on. We'll work together and let your mom and Aunt Beth render the tallow."

"They don't give much light anyway," Tommy still grumbled.

Emily laughed at him. "I can knit with my eyes closed, so if we run out of candles, I'll still make you socks."

She picked up one end of a thin strip of cloth. "You hold the other end, and we'll twist."

"As soon as you have six of those, we'll pour the first batch," Sally told them. She set the mold on the table. "See," she said, pointing to the hole in the bottom of each section. "You tie a knot in the end of a wick and pull it through the hole. Then you tie the other end to a stick to hold the wick straight while you pour."

"I'll go find the sticks," Tommy said eagerly.

"You go, and I'll make wicks," Emily told him as he dashed off, letting the end of the one they were working on unravel. She shook her head and started winding again. "Is this tight enough, Sally?"

"You do a better job than that son of mine. He can't sit still." Sally chuckled.

Beth peeked in the door. "This bear fat is about melted."

"Keep stirring," Sally called to her. "We don't have enough wicks to make a pour yet."

"We still have a lot of meat in the cooler by the creek. Would you like to cook some up for Sunday?" Emily asked as she continued to wind small strips of cloth into wicks.

"That sounds good," Sally said as she fit the first wick into the mold. "You have to keep these straight, or you don't get a good candle."

"How many more things do I need to learn to live in this place?" Emily grumbled.

"You sound like Tommy," her sister called from the door. "You could go home and marry Henry Richards and never have to make another candle."

"You are cruel, Beth Miller. You know I would rather die before I'd marry that horrid man."

"What's this all about?" Sally asked as she tied another wick.

Emily told Sally about the man back in Ashford. "My mother has made up her mind that I'm to marry that man. I don't know why she hates me so much."

"Emmy, she doesn't hate you," Beth said as she brought a pot of tea from the fire. "She thinks you should be married to a store owner instead of a frontiersman."

"I won't let that happen," Emily declared.

After the first candles were poured, the women put together a meal of bear stew and vegetables.

"Papa says we can stay the night," Tommy announced, holding out his plate for a second helping.

"Do you want to sleep outside with me?" Jonathan asked the little boy.

"Please, Mama—may I?"

She nodded, and he shot off the bench to run after Jonathan.

"He's getting so big," Sally said wistfully.

Just then Beth stood up from the table. "Let's get these dishes cleaned up so we can sit outside in the cool breeze."

Emily joined the others after putting the rest of the stew into the box by the creek. She heard the men talking about going for salt and wondered if a letter from her father would be at Colosse when they arrived there.

The next day the women poured another six candles.

"I'll leave the mold now that you know what to do," Sally told them.

"We'll return it with candles for you," Beth promised.

Mr. Miller was standing by the door, holding a haunch of bear. "Can you use this much meat, Sally?"

"I'll cook up most of it for the fellowship on Sunday."

"Can we eat some too?" Tommy asked. "I liked Miss Emily's stew."

Emily hugged the child. "Thank you for teaching me to make wicks."

He grinned. "You make them so well that I won't have to any more."

&

Sally's stew was as popular at the fellowship meeting as Emily's had been at supper.

"The Lord has provided well for us," Pastor Barnes said, after finishing a second helping. Turning to Jonathan, he asked quietly, "Did you receive an answer from Mr. Goodman yet?"

"No," Jonathan answered, "but I hope it comes soon." He looked over at Emily who was helping the other women clear away the dishes.

"I'll be around these parts till the snow flies, so we can have a wedding whenever you say," the pastor said.

A few minutes later, Mr. Wheeler approached the Miller brothers. "I hear you boys are going after salt. If you can bring back any extra, I'd be interested in buying it."

This started several of the men asking about David and Jonathan's proposed trip to Onondaga Lake.

"I took a wagon there last year," Ned Drumhill said. "I could have sold all of what I returned with. I should have made a second trip, but we had too much to do here."

"How long were you on the road?" David asked.

"I have only one ox, so it took me over two weeks to go round trip."

They discussed the price. "It's a lot cheaper to buy where they mine it than to go to Oswego or even Rotterdam. Now that Jonathan can grind our corn, I don't have to make the trip to the gristmill in Rotterdam. Can you bring me some salt too?" Joshua Crandell asked.

"Beth won't want me to be gone so long," David told his brother as they pulled the Indian cart home.

"We could make one trip for salt, come home, then go for a second load later," Jonathan suggested.

"We could make a nice profit, you know, and buy or barter for more of the things we need," David mused.

"With two oxen, we should be able to make the trip down and back in ten days."

"Are you thinking we should borrow Pa's ox and take two wagons?"

"Pa's using it. He's still trying to get hay in," Jonathan reminded his brother.

"Your idea about making more than one trip sounds good then."

"You sound like a merchant. Let's not say anything to the women yet. We should ask Pa what he thinks. He'll be the one left to keep both places going."

"We can't leave till we smoke all the meat anyway. That'll give us time to plan this out."

thirteen

"Two weeks!" Beth nearly screamed. "You can't leave us alone for two weeks!"

"Pa will come to check on you. If you need him, you'll have Jonathan's mare to ride to Sally's." David tried to calm his wife.

Emily came up behind her sister and put her arms around her. "We can do it, Beth. We have the garden to harvest, so we'll be too busy to know they're gone." She spoke the words but did not believe them. *I miss Jonathan anytime we are apart.*

"How soon do you leave?" Beth asked in a quieter tone.

"As soon as the meat is smoked, we'll store it and leave. It may take us only ten or eleven days to get back."

"We'd better start getting food ready for you to take. Will the bear jerky be ready?" Emily asked.

"I just took some out of the smoker to try," Jonathan said, coming through the door with a pan of dried meat.

"It looks like shoe leather." Emily wrinkled her nose.

Jonathan laughed. "It will keep us from going hungry when we're on the road."

"I'll bake up some corn bread that will taste better. At least until it dries up," she added wryly.

"Then we'll soak it in coffee," Jonathan told her, smiling into her eyes.

His look made her wish he would stay home. But living so close sometimes became a torment. *I pray for the day we will have a place of our own. Please, Lord, let Father's letter be waiting.*

❧

The wagon's load would be light going out, with only a few

provisions and a canvas to put over the salt to keep it dry on the way home.

"We should make good time," David told his brother as they pulled out of the yard.

Jonathan looked back at the sisters standing in the doorway. "Maybe there will be a letter at Colosse."

"Emily's father has had plenty of time to answer you. Is your cabin ready to move into?"

"It lacks only a few things being finished. I hope to get some dishes for Emily on this trip."

David laughed. "You're not waiting for her parents' blessing?"

"She won't marry without hearing from her father. She quotes the commandment to honor her parents every time I suggest it."

The oxen plodded along at a good pace. The men were in Colosse before lunchtime.

"I have some letters for the Millers," the innkeeper told them when they inquired about the mail.

Jonathan took them eagerly. Puzzled, he handed one to David. "This is for you. Why would Mr. Goodman write to you?"

"I married his daughter," David reminded his brother. "Is the other one for you?"

Jonathan shook his head. "It's for Emily, but the handwriting is the same."

David tore open his letter. Jonathan watched his brother's expression turn to disbelief as he read.

"This is terrible. The girls' father accuses me of holding Emily and making her a nursemaid. He insists I bring her back at once and complains he has to hire a woman to care for his wife when Emily should do it." David looked up. "This does not sound like Edward Goodman. He's always been kind to us. He gave us all sorts of goods plus the sledge and oxen when we came out here. Why would he change now?"

Jonathan looked at the letter in his hand. "I don't want to

give this to Emily if it is more of the same."

"What will she do?"

"If she believes this is what her father wants, I fear she will go back to Ashford," Jonathan said, scarcely able to utter the words.

Just then a guest at the inn stepped forward. "Say! I hear you men are going for salt."

"That's right," David told the man. "We're bringing back a wagonload for us and for some of our neighbors."

"I would pay well if you'd bring a load back here. I only have a small cart and a horse, but if I had salt, I could peddle it to the farmers around these parts."

David looked at Jonathan. "What do you think?"

"What are you offering?" Jonathan asked the man. The extra cash would help if he had to go back east to talk to Emily's father.

The man negotiated with the Millers to settle on a fair price, and the innkeeper agreed to allow the man to store salt at his place until he could sell it all.

"I'll take a few bags myself," the innkeeper added.

"My brother and I will need to talk about this," David told the innkeeper. "Perhaps you could serve us a meal while we think it over."

"What do you think?" David asked Jonathan again, as he dug into the hearty stew before him.

"I think the merchant in you is coming out," Jonathan said with a grin. "What about the women? If we're gone more than two weeks, they'll worry."

"They can manage a few days extra. We can leave word with the innkeeper to ask anyone going that way to let them know we're making two trips. They'll understand."

"It'll be almost time to harvest the corn before we get back," Jonathan reminded David.

"With the good Lord's help we can do it," David declared.

They shook hands with both the peddler and the innkeeper

over the deal and started back on the road.

"Next year we should do the peddling ourselves," David suggested.

Jonathan flicked the reins over the back of the oxen. "You'll have that mercantile yet."

"I've been thinking about writing to Mr. Richards. He could tell me how to find goods to sell."

"Speaking of writing, may I see that letter from Mr. Goodman?"

David pulled it out of his pocket. "Are you trying to decide what to do?"

Jonathan nodded as he read the letter. "Emily let me read the last letter she received from her mother. This handwriting looks the same." He turned to his brother. "David, Mr. Goodman didn't write this letter! Mrs. Goodman did!"

"Why would she do that?"

"I think the woman isn't well somehow. She writes terrible things to Emily and upsets her," he said sharply, with anger rising in his voice.

"I thought it was strange when Mr. Goodman gave us the wagon and the goods but told us not to say anything to his wife," David told his brother.

"I wonder if he ever saw the letter I wrote." Jonathan drove on in silence. "When you write to Mr. Richards would you let me put another letter to Mr. Goodman in with it? Mr. Richards would see that it got to the right person."

"Do you really think Mrs. Goodman would hold back mail addressed to her husband?"

"I put nothing past that woman now."

"We'll send the packet when we come back with the first load of salt," David assured his brother.

"I don't like to do it, but I'll have to give Emily the letter we picked up." He sighed. "Maybe it will help if I tell her I've written to her father again. What will you do with the letter you received?"

"Burn it," David stated firmly.

Emily and Beth gathered the garden vegetables. They dried some of the onions, and after digging the carrots, they put them in bins David's father had made for the root cellar.

"We'll have to spend a day or two at Jonathan's place to dig the potatoes. How will we bring them back here?" Emily asked.

"Shouldn't we put some of this in the root cellar at Jonathan's?"

"I don't know. We'd better keep it all here until we get a letter from Father. If Jonathan and I get married and move, we can take some provisions then."

"Don't you mean *when* you get married? I don't know why you insist on waiting for Father's permission. You're a grown woman and should be able to make up your own mind."

Emily leaned on the shovel she had been using to dig carrots. "Honor thy father. . . ," she said wistfully. "I just can't start a marriage by breaking the commandments." She pushed the shovel into the ground with vigor.

"You have my permission, and I'm your only relative here," Beth reasoned. "Have you talked to Pastor Barnes about this?"

"He can't change the commandments. To be right with the Lord, I have to obey." Emily turned over a shovelful of dirt and carrots. "Besides, I owe Father that much after the way I left home."

"Even if it means you have to give up Jonathan?"

Emily sighed. "I can't give him up. I love him, and I want to stay here and make a home with him." She moved to dig another row of carrots.

"You can't have it both ways," Beth reminded her, picking up the carrots her sister had unearthed.

"I keep praying we'll hear from Father. I don't know why it's taking so long."

"He's probably arguing with Mother," Beth said, piling carrots in a bucket.

"I can't imagine that. He never speaks a cross word to her." Emily plunged the shovel into the ground again.

"Then you can imagine how hard it is for him to convince Mother to let you marry Jonathan instead of Henry Richards." Beth picked up the full bucket to carry back to the waiting bin.

"Let me carry that bucket for you," Emily said, taking the carrots from her sister. "This will about fill the first bin. We have so much produce we may have to use the other root cellar."

"Don't forget we need to give enough to Sally and Papa Miller for the winter," Beth reminded Emily.

"They have to harvest all that corn." Emily straightened her back and stretched to take some of the stiffness away. "How much longer before the men come back? We'll need their help."

Beth sighed. "It's been almost two weeks. They should be back any day now. Oh, I hear Phillip crying!" She ran for the cabin.

⁊⦆

Two weeks passed with no sign of David and Jonathan.

"What can we do?" Beth asked her father-in-law, who had come to check on them.

"Now, Elizabeth, they are grown men and can take care of themselves. Maybe it was farther to the salt mines than they were told."

"Should we send someone to look for them?" Emily asked.

"Not yet. Give them another week," he said gently.

"Another week!" Beth cried.

"Why don't you girls spend some time with Sally? It will make the days go faster."

"We really need to harvest this vegetable garden," Emily told him. "We filled a bin of potatoes for you and Sally and left it at Jonathan's because we're running out of room here.

There will be other things too."

"I'll bring my small wagon over to pick them up. I've improved the root cellar at our place. If I come tomorrow, will you come home with me?"

Emily noticed the sad expression on her sister's face. "We need a day of rest," she declared, "and I need to return Sally's candle mold with some candles."

The day's visit to Sally helped, but still the time passed with no word from the men.

The week dragged on. The sisters stopped talking about how long it had been. They each had burned the count into their minds.

"It's been three weeks now. Don't you think we should do something?" Beth asked her father-in-law.

"I'll talk to Colonel Dewey, since he seems to know everything that's going on in these parts. He'll tell us what to do."

Beth sighed, and Emily reached out to put her arm around her.

"Everything will turn out all right. We'll just make sure they take us with them when they go for salt next year," she said, smiling.

"And who will do the work here?" Beth asked, picking up the beets she had just pulled.

"Let's take a break for tea. At least with the men gone, we don't have much cooking to do." Emily coaxed her sister back to the cabin.

Later, after tea, Emily could hear a horse entering the yard. "Someone's coming!" She ran outside. "Oh, it's just Mr. Miller coming back."

The women greeted him at the door. "What did you find out? Are they all right?" they both asked at once.

"I met Colonel Dewey on his way over here. One of his sons had been to Colosse and brought back a message for you. It seems our boys plan to make two trips to the mines. They had sold a load of salt before they even left Colosse."

He took the cup of tea Emily offered him. "That David is a natural-born salesman." His voice held a note of pride. "I'm only sorry it took so long for the message to get to you. But they should be back any day now."

Two days later the oxen pulled a loaded wagon into the yard.

"Thank God!" Beth said as she ran to her husband's arms.

Emily looked at Jonathan. *I wish he would hug me like that.*

"Come and see what we've brought you," Jonathan said, interrupting her thoughts. He reached up and pulled a squawking crate out of the wagon bed. "We'll have to make a coop real fast for these."

"Are those chickens? You mean we'll have eggs?"

Jonathan beamed at her pleasure. Next he set down a box and told her to open it.

She pulled off the wrappings and peered inside. "Dishes? For me?" she asked in disbelief.

"I told you I would bring you dishes for those shelves in our cabin." He smiled into her eyes.

Our cabin. Her heart raced. "Did you hear from Father?" she asked eagerly. Her joy faded when she saw Jonathan's grim look.

"No, I didn't. There's a letter for you, but we'll read it together later," he said, turning away from her. "I need to unhook the oxen."

David had his arm around Beth's waist and led her to the wagon. "Let me show you what I brought our son." He reached into a box behind the seat and pulled out a ball of black and white fur. "Our boy needs a dog to grow up with."

"And our little stepbrother needs one too," Jonathan said, returning from the barn. He pulled a second puppy out of the box.

With the excitement of the gifts, the women forgot to be angry at being left alone so long.

"What about the letter?" Emily asked Jonathan after the wagon had been unloaded and Beth had started supper.

Jonathan pulled it out of his pocket.

"Is it from Father?" she asked.

"I don't think so," he said quietly.

Emily looked puzzled and opened the packet. "This is my mother's handwriting." As she read the words, she felt faint and welcomed Jonathan's arm around her. "She has signed my father's name," said Emily sharply, pulling away from Jonathan, the color rising in her cheeks.

"I don't think your father knows anything about this."

"Why? Did you get a letter too?"

"No, David did. We read it together and fear your father has not seen any of the messages we've sent him. I've written him again."

"Why do you think he'll get this one?" Emily demanded.

"Because we sent it to Mr. Richards and asked him to give it to your father."

"So we must still wait." Emily sighed, collapsing back into his arms. "How long will it be?"

fourteen

Jonathan held Emily close to his heart. "Why must we wait, Emily? Why do you honor that woman? She is deceitful. She accuses my brother of holding you hostage," he said angrily. "She's written a letter and signed your father's name. She is cruel to you."

Emily stepped away from him, her head down, and spoke in a whisper. "She is my mother. I am duty bound to show her respect if for no other reason than she is my father's wife." She looked up at Jonathan, pleading with him to understand. "I love my father, and I can't do anything that will hurt him. Please—can't we wait till we hear from him?"

Jonathan sighed. "I don't know what more I can do. I want to marry you, and I have done everything I can think of to make that marriage honorable. It is up to you." He turned away from her and walked to where his brother was chopping wood.

"I can't reason with her," he told his brother in a tone of despair.

"So she insists on waiting?"

Jonathan nodded. "There's no reason to start that barn at my place, unless you think I should move over there."

"I'm not going to kick you out. Beth and I will miss you and Emily when you do move to your own place. Besides, it's too late in the year to start a barn." David tossed another chunk of firewood on the stack.

"If we don't build the barn now, what will we do with the corn and fodder?"

"We've got a big stack of bark. Let's put up a pole frame and tie on the bark for a shelter. Pa's got his barn ready, so he'll take enough of the corn stalks for his oxen this winter." David bent to set up another log to chop.

"With his ox out of this barn, I found room in a corner for a chicken coop. The pigs will be all right where they are until we butcher," Jonathan reasoned out loud.

David clamped his hand on his brother's shoulder. "Let's go to work."

≈

Emily struggled with her confusion. *Honor thy father and thy mother.* Over and over the words echoed in her mind. *I may not have always respected Mother, but I have tried to obey her. And marriage is such an important decision.*

Jonathan is right—she is deceitful. She has lied and plotted against me. Dear God, do I still owe her honor?

Beth took the shirt Emily had wrung out over the washtub and hung it to dry. "Is that the last?"

Emily nodded. "There isn't much reason to dump this water on the garden. It's about finished."

"Why don't we take the dishes Jonathan brought you over to your cabin?"

"Beth, it isn't my cabin," Emily said in exasperation.

"Do you insist on waiting?" Beth asked.

Emily sighed. "I don't know what to do. I keep thinking of the commandment to honor our parents."

"Don't you think our mother should honor us? Doesn't it work both ways?" Beth asked with sudden bitterness in her voice. "I can't believe the lies she wrote about my husband."

"I've read the Bible over and over—how parents must discipline their children. I guess she thinks what she is doing is disciplining me for being rather headstrong."

"I don't believe that, Emmy. Our mother has done a wicked thing. She accuses my husband of holding you hostage. I can love her because she is my mother, but I don't have to approve of what she does. If that means I don't honor her, so be it!" Beth banged the empty washtub against the side of the cabin.

Emily felt the tears welling up in her eyes. "I love Jonathan, and I want to marry him. It's all I've ever wanted. But I don't know what to do about Mother and getting Father's blessing."

Beth dried her hands on her apron. "We have the fellowship on Sunday. Will you talk to Pastor Barnes?"

Emily smiled despite her tears. "Is this your way of saying I won't listen to my family but maybe I will listen to the pastor?"

"Yes, I guess it is. We are your family, and we think we know what is best for you. How long do you think you can keep Jonathan waiting?" Beth asked.

"I think he's angry with me."

"Does that surprise you?" Beth put her arm around her sister. "If you go back home, will you take all the things you have here?"

Emily thought of Henry Richards, and her stomach turned sour. She could only shake her head no.

"Then give them to Jonathan. Let's put some of the things you've made into his cabin. Then if you decide to marry him, they will be there waiting for you." Beth hugged her sister and stepped back. "For one thing, we need to get that rug you keep enlarging out of our cabin. If you make it any bigger it won't fit in Jonathan's cabin either," she teased.

"Don't you think I should ask Jonathan first?" Emily asked. "If I go back east, he may not want anything I've made."

"Then he can give the things away after you're gone."

Emily nodded her head sadly. "All right. I'll go hitch up the Indian cart. Should we tell the men where we are?"

"They're busy cutting poles. They only need one ox to move limbs, and we'll be back before they come looking for a meal," Beth said. "Will you put Pepper in his pen? He might try to follow us," she called back to her sister as she started for the cabin.

Emily laughed. "Phillip will have to learn to walk now. That puppy thinks anything on all fours is a playmate." She reached down to where the puppy and the infant had discovered the mud from the wash water. When she picked up the furry black dog, he licked the salty tears from her face.

"Put these in too," Beth said, carrying three quilts from the cabin.

"Those are from my hope chest."

"That's right. We brought these out with us. Where is your set of linen sheets?"

"In the bottom of my trunk. They aren't in the way there."

"Oh, that's good. Well, let me tuck Phillip in the cart, and we'll be off."

The women led the ox to Jonathan's cabin.

"Where is the root cellar?" Beth asked as she picked up Phillip.

"It's covered by a trap door now, so your son is safe." Emily pulled the quilts out of the cart and started for the cabin. Inside, she dropped the quilts on the rough-hewn floor and opened the shutters. The sun shone through the window Jonathan had installed.

"We could use the breeze today," Beth said, putting her son on the floor. "But it will be nice in the winter to have more light. David will put our window in as soon as it starts to get cold."

"I don't know where to put the quilts," Emily said as she picked them off the floor.

Beth looked around. "You don't have a bed yet. Why, you don't even have a table and benches!"

"It doesn't look as if they'll be needed for awhile," Emily said sadly.

"Pile those quilts in a corner, and help me get the rug."

They carried the rag rug into the cabin and spread it in front of the fireplace.

"It's big," Emily admitted.

"You'll need to make a smaller one to put by the bed. The floor is cold in the winter."

Emily felt her face redden at her sister's mention of a bed in Jonathan's cabin. "I'll bring in the box of dishes," she said, pointing toward the opposite wall. "They'll look nice on the shelves he's made."

Emily felt better after putting the things in Jonathan's cabin. It made it easier to dream of it being her home one day too.

During the next few days she stayed busy with baking and cleaning for the Sunday fellowship and didn't have time to brood over her dilemma.

After the sermon and discussion of the Scriptures on Sunday, Emily approached Pastor Barnes. "May I talk with you, please?"

He smiled warmly at her. "I hope it's about your wedding."

Emily sighed. "It is, but not to set a date."

"Let's get a plate of food and sit in the shade," he suggested.

Emily followed him to the table and picked up a plate. She put a few things on hers, while Pastor Barnes piled the food high on his. "Women around here are good cooks. I keep telling my son-in-law he should move here. You need a full-time preacher, and he also tans hides and makes shoes."

"We need a shoemaker, for certain. We try to keep the children in moccasins, but our leather is stiff and hard to work with," she said, following the pastor away from the food.

"Let's sit over here." He pointed to a spot under a large tree.

Once they were seated and the pastor started eating, Emily told him about the letters to her and David. "I don't know what to do. The Millers don't think my father has even seen the messages we have sent." She looked down. "My mother is not a good woman. She wants me to marry a man I find repulsive, and she's doing everything she can to make it happen—even lying about David by saying he's holding me hostage." Emily avoided looking at the pastor when she talked about her mother.

"I don't think it's an unfair judgment to say she is wrong in what she's doing," Pastor Barnes said firmly.

"But must I still honor her?" Emily looked up now, no longer afraid to meet his gentle gaze.

Pastor Barnes put his plate down. "It is your father's blessing you seek?"

"Yes," she told him.

"Is there no way you can write directly to him?"

"David and Jonathan wrote letters and sent them to the man David used to work for. They asked him to take them to my father." Emily looked down again, feeling ashamed of the need to go around her mother.

"Then if you still feel you must have his blessing, you'd better wait until you hear from your father." He patted Emily on the shoulder. "If you'll give me the name of the pastor of your church in Ashford, I'll write to him for you."

"I would be grateful if you would," she said, her voice brightening. "My sister and the Millers think I'm wrong to make Jonathan wait for my father's blessing, but I'll feel better if I know I have tried every way to contact him."

"The message to your pastor will go out tomorrow. I'll stay here until the snow flies, you know, then I'll winter near Rotterdam with my daughter and her husband. When you hear from your father, send one of Colonel Dewey's sons to find me. We'll have a wedding as soon as I can get here."

"Thank you." Emily set her untouched plate on the ground where Pepper could eat it and watched Pastor Barnes cross the yard to speak to Jonathan.

❧

"Will she agree to marry me?" Jonathan asked the pastor.

He shook his head. "She feels so strongly, I think you'd better allow time for her father to respond to you. I fear if she marries you now because of the pressure we put on her and finds out later her father did object, the guilt would torment her severely."

"I hope his letter comes before winter. David and I have talked, and if I don't hear, I'll try to go east right after

Christmas. I should be able to make the trip and be back before the sap runs."

Pastor Barnes nodded. "That sounds like a good plan. I know it's hard to wait, but you want a happy bride. You know I keep both of you in my prayers."

"Thank you for that. I find it sad that one woman can cause so much grief."

❧

After completing the pole building, the men started harvesting the corn. "We have to pick the ears first. Then we'll go back and cut the stalks for the oxen to eat in the winter," George Miller explained to the women.

"How can we help?" Emily asked.

"You'll husk corn, probably until your fingers bleed," he told them with a smile. "We have to shuck the corn we plan to grind into meal. What we save for the animals we can husk as we need it."

"We have to shuck it too?" Beth asked.

"We have a grinder to do that. You put the ear in and grind the handle until it scrapes the kernels off the cob."

"That sounds like a lot of work for johnnycake," Emily said with a grin.

"You forget I have to sit on that stump and pound for hours to grind the kernels into meal," Jonathan reminded her.

"I appreciate how hard you work," Emily said softly.

"When do we start this project?" Beth asked her father-in-law.

"Tomorrow. The boys will bring the wagon over so you can ride. They'll need the wagon to carry the corn. I hope it's so full coming back that you have to walk." He chuckled.

"I'm not sure I like that plan, but we do eat a lot of johnnycake," Emily said. "Maybe we can get Harriet Wheeler to teach us her song. If we sing while we husk corn, the time will go faster." *Maybe the time won't drag so much until we hear from Father either,* she added to herself.

fifteen

David, Jonathan, and their father pulled the ears of corn from the stalks. Emily looked at the rising pile they dumped by Sally's cabin. "This is going to take days," she moaned.

Sally laughed. "When I lived on a farm in Connecticut we had husking bees. All the young people would gather at someone's barn to husk the corn."

"Why would they do that?" Emily asked.

"The secret is that if you husk a red ear you get to kiss your best beau."

Emily felt the warmth stealing into her cheeks. "I don't think we have any red ears," she stammered.

"You'll have to keep husking and find out," Beth said with a smile.

"Are the children all right?" Sally asked as she picked up another ear of corn.

"They're playing with the puppies. Phillip is trying to walk. He takes two steps and sits down, and Pepper gets right on top of him. David did a good thing to bring the pups home."

"Tommy has his own Rover now. He thinks all dogs should be named Rover. I guess I should be grateful God guided the Wheelers' Rover when I needed Polly's help."

The women piled the husks into a stack and the corn into the wagon. "Mr. Miller was right. My hands are getting sore," Emily complained.

"I think of the winter my poor ox had nothing to eat but tree branches. It keeps me working. He'll eat well this winter."

"Is Papa Miller still going to buy a cow?" Beth asked, tossing an ear of corn on the growing pile.

"He says he'll take the ashes to Fort Ontario to sell. After he pays on the mortgage, he'll look for a cow."

"We'll bring you eggs and take back milk," Beth told her.

"I'll make cheese too," Sally said. "I watched my aunt, and I think I can remember what she did."

"God is good to us," Emily pointed out. "We're living off the bounty of His land."

Sally nodded. "It sure beats boiled salt fish and a bit of cornmeal. I'll always be thankful to the Lord for sending George to care for the children and me."

After harvesting the corn, the men cut the stalks to be used as fodder. The six adults worked long and hard to take care of the food they had grown. The children and puppies enjoyed the sunshine and each other.

"When we finish with the corn, we should take a day to gather nuts," Sally told them. She looked at her hands, swollen and sore from the work. "And if you think husking corn is messy, wait until you see what black walnut husks do to your hands."

"Is it worse than this?" Emily asked, with a twinge of concern.

"Oh, you won't be sore, but you'll be stained. I found last year that if I washed in the mud at the creek, it took some of the black sticky stuff off my hands."

"You could be having tea with Mrs. Gardner," Beth told her sister, with a twinkle in her eyes.

"Just show me the walnut trees," Emily said firmly.

❧

The corn for grinding had been taken to David and Beth's cabin.

"How does this stump mill work?" David asked his brother.

"You shuck some of those ears of corn while I make sure the hollow in the stump is clean." With the wooden bowl piled with kernels, Jonathan perched on the stump and pounded until he had ground the kernels into meal.

"Show me how it works," David said. "We can take turns

so it isn't so much work for just one."

Emily came outside to watch. "Are you going to grind all that corn?" She glanced at the wagonload standing in the yard.

Jonathan looked down from his perch on the stump grinder. "How much cornmeal will you need next winter?"

"A lot," Emily admitted. "Can I help shuck?"

"Here—I'll show you how it works," David offered.

The three worked together, filling the sacks of meal.

Sometime later, Emily stood up to rest her back and wipe the perspiration from her forehead. "Someone is coming," she said, pointing toward the path.

Douglas Wheeler strode into the yard. "I see you have the grinder up and working. I came to ask about getting some corn ground."

Jonathan stopped pounding to greet their neighbor.

Mr. Wheeler looked at the wagonload of corn. "It looks as if it will be awhile before you can get to me. I need to barter with you too."

"I'll go and make some coffee," Emily said and hurried to the cabin where Beth had been working inside.

"I already owe you for the salt you brought me. Now I have corn to grind," Mr. Wheeler stated.

David pointed to the hog pen. "We'll enjoy your pigs this winter. Is there any chance we could get a couple more in the spring?"

"But I'll still owe for the salt."

"You have big strapping sons. Send them over with the corn, and they can use the grinder to make the meal you need," Jonathan told the man.

"That would be right neighborly of you," Mr. Wheeler said with a smile.

"You helped Pa with his barn, and I plan to build a barn at my place next year," Jonathan said.

The men sat on upturned logs and enjoyed the coffee Emily brought them. They continued to discuss their plans and exchange ideas until Mr. Wheeler stood to leave.

"I'll let you know when we have our corn ground so your boys can start on yours," Jonathan said.

"And I'll let you know when to pick up a couple of piglets in the spring," Mr. Wheeler replied, extending his hand to shake on the deal.

❧

Emily sat down on a bench inside the cabin to watch her sister sew a shirt for Phillip. "I get tired working outside with Jonathan, but I like to be near him."

"I should do more to help outside, but there's so much to do here. Phillip keeps outgrowing his clothes, and David keeps wearing out his socks."

"I look forward to needing to do those tasks," Emily said wistfully. "You'll have to show me how to cut out small shirts. I made Phillip baby clothes, but regular boy shirts will be different."

"Make one for Jonathan," Beth suggested.

Emily felt her face grow hot. "Do you think it's all right, Beth? And besides, how would I measure him for a shirt?"

"The man needs clothes, and you can sew. You could use one of his old ones to take measurements. What wouldn't be all right about that?" Beth asked.

"What about cloth?"

"We still have some homespun David got in trade for salt, and it's one of the things his father is to bring back. The list keeps getting longer. I don't think we'll have extra to pay on the mortgage this year," she added, a sudden note of concern in her voice.

"We can pay the interest. We have a good cabin and lots of food. Thank God for what He has given us."

"You're right, Emmy. Keep reminding me of my blessings," Beth told her sister. "I dread the day you move. It's wonderful to have you with me all the time."

Emily frowned. "It doesn't look as if you have anything to

worry about for awhile."

The men finished their coffee and brought the mugs back to the cabin. Mr. Wheeler stuck his head in the door. "By the way, Polly sends her greetings and says she'll see you on Sunday," he told the sisters.

"We're looking forward to it," Beth replied. "We'll be snow-bound soon enough."

Mr. Wheeler left, and the men returned to the stump grinder. Emily rose from the bench with a sigh and walked outside to shuck more corn. David carried the cobs to the new pole building.

"What are these for?" Emily asked.

"The oxen will chew on them in the winter," he explained.

❧

The brothers took a day away from the corn to help their father load up the barrels of ash for the trip to Fort Ontario.

"You sure you don't mind going alone?" Jonathan asked.

"I'll be fine. I can make it there in a day." Father smiled. "I may have to take an extra day to bargain for all the things on the list the girls are sending with me."

"Will there be enough money?" David asked.

"We have the extra from selling salt. If we get our nine cents a barrel for ashes, we'll pay the interest and lay in supplies for the winter. I hope the price of coffee hasn't gone up again, though."

David turned to his brother. "How much will you need if you go east?"

"What's this?" their father asked. "Are you going to desert us?"

"No, Pa, but if I don't hear from Emily's father by Christmas, I'll make a trip back to see him. I'm sure I can be back in time to help with the syrup season." He turned to his brother. "I won't need much money. If I have to, I'll camp out and not pay lodging."

"You really love that girl, don't you, Son?" Father clapped

his work-worn hand on Jonathan's shoulder.

"Yes, I do." He sighed and gazed out across the field. Turning back, he said, "Let's get the last of these barrels stowed so you can take off tomorrow. It looks as if the weather will hold." He glanced up at the sky. "The cold wet mornings seem to be coming earlier this year. I wouldn't be surprised to see frost one of these days."

"We'll keep an eye on Sally and the children while you're gone," David promised.

"That Tommy is real disappointed not to go with me. I told him he could go next year."

Emily came to check on the progress and heard this last. "If he goes, you'll have to take his dog."

"That's how I got him to stay home this time. I told him Rover couldn't come, and he wouldn't leave his pup." Father chuckled.

"Beth and I will go over to visit Sally. She's supposed to take us out to gather nuts."

"You'd better do it soon. This Indian summer won't last much longer," Father warned.

❧

Beth and Emily loaded Phillip and Pepper in the Indian cart and headed for Sally's the day after George Miller left for the fort.

"Let's have a cup of tea first, then we'll go out to the walnut trees," Sally told them.

Later, as the children and dogs romped in the fallen leaves, the women searched for black walnuts. "Now you know where they got their name." Sally laughed and held up a black-stained hand.

"What do we do with them now?" Emily asked.

"They need to dry, then the husk will come off. After that, we can store the nuts for winter."

"Dry them how?" Beth asked.

"I spread them in the sun until the weather gets bad. Then I put them by the side of the fireplace."

"I can see Phillip and Pepper! They'll think they have a whole pile of new toys," Beth moaned.

"We'd better get a box to put them in," Emily suggested.

"If we pile these in the cart, where will we put Phillip and the dog?"

"First, let's go by the creek and see if Sally's mud will clean off some of this black goo."

When they arrived at the creek, Emily pulled off her shoes and hiked up her skirt to wade in the water.

"You're worse than the children," Beth complained. She reached out to stop her son from sitting down in the water with all his clothes on.

"I'm looking at the fish," Emily said, then turned to Sally. "Are those salmon?"

"It looks like it to me. We'd better plan a day of catching salmon to salt," Sally said, following Emily into the water.

"Look, Mommy!" Tommy called out, trapping a fish in the shallows and pushing it up on the shore. "I can catch them in my hands!"

"Let's get these nuts laid out to dry. We'll need to spend a day in the creek," Sally told them. "George will be back in a few days. I'll come over tomorrow or the next day or so, if the weather holds. I'll be able to greet him with fresh salmon when he gets back."

"You'll have to show us how to catch salmon," Emily said.

"Tommy just did." Sally laughed.

sixteen

The Indian summer continued. Sally arrived early one morning at Beth's cabin.

"The sun will be hot by noon. It will feel good when we're in the creek," she said, taking a cup of coffee from Emily.

"Is it safe to take the children?" Beth asked.

"We'll have to watch Phillip and Abbie, but Tommy will be a big help. We'd best leave the dogs home. They would just splash in the water and scatter the salmon."

Emily joined Sally and Beth at the table with her cup of coffee. "Now explain what we're going to do."

Sally set her cup down. "The creek is filled with fish. So we herd them into the shallows and, as Tommy did yesterday, toss them on the sand." She turned to Beth. "Why don't you stay on the shore with the little ones, and as we throw the fish on the bank, you can hit them on the head and pile them in one place."

"Hit them on the head?" Beth stared at Sally.

"It will keep them from flopping right back into the water."

Emily giggled. "This sounds like quite an adventure. I've never been fishing, and now you say we're going to catch them in our hands?"

"When you're wet and your feet feel like ice, you won't think it's fun any more," Sally warned.

"Well, so far husking corn and picking up black walnuts have been a challenge. Let's go fishing!" she exclaimed, gathering the empty cups to wash.

They tucked the children into the Indian cart and left to the sound of the puppies howling from their pen. Tommy looked very glum. "I don't know why Rover has to stay home," he grumbled.

"Because he wouldn't stay out of the water, and he would scare off all the fish," his mother told him, running her fingers through his bright curls. "We need you to show us how to catch the salmon in our hands."

They stopped at a spot where the creek had widened and the water ran shallow.

Emily pointed to the water. "Look at that! You could almost walk across the creek on fish!"

"Their fins are sticking out of the water!" Beth exclaimed.

"Find yourself a rock, Beth, and we'll see if we can throw you some fish," Sally said, lifting Abbie out of the cart. "Now you must mind Aunt Beth, Abbie. Mommy has to be in the water, but it's cold, and you wouldn't like it."

Abbie didn't look convinced, but she stood next to Beth with her thumb in her mouth. Phillip yelled to get out of the cart and toddled over to stand by Abbie until he saw a bug on the ground and dropped to his hands and knees to follow it.

"Once Emily gets the idea of catching fish, I'll come and help with the children," Sally promised Beth.

"Look, Mommy!" Tommy yelled. He already had his pants rolled up and his shoes off. He managed to get a slippery salmon on dry land. His mother ran to grab it and toss it up on the bank.

"Well, I guess I can do that," Emily declared, taking off her shoes and stockings. She tucked her skirt into the top of her apron and waded into the water. She squealed as fish shot in every direction.

"Stand still, Miss Emily. They'll come back," Tommy called.

Emily watched the boy. He stood just outside a shallow at the edge of the creek. When the fish swam toward him, he blocked the straight path so some of them entered the shallow water. Then he quickly grabbed for them and tossed them to dry land.

Emily found her own little curve in the creek bed with a shallow spot near shore. It took several tries, but finally she yelled in victory as she managed to get a salmon to shore.

Sally waded into the creek and started grabbing fish.

"I can't keep up!" Beth called out to them as she tried to club the fish and throw them higher on the bank.

"Just don't let them back in the water," Sally called back. "It looks as if Emily and Tommy are doing well. I'll get a few more and come and help you."

"All right," Beth said as she tried to pick up two more fish by the gills and carry them to the pile she had started. Suddenly she looked around her.

"Abbie, what happened to Phillip?"

The little girl was sitting on the ground pulling at blades of grass. She shook her head.

Beth turned back toward the creek and screamed. Dashing to the water she pointed frantically to Phillip who lay face down in the water.

"I'll get him!" Emily shouted as she plunged through the water to grab the child up into her arms.

Phillip came up coughing and spitting up water. As soon as he got his wind, he started to cry.

"He's all yours!" Emily said, handing the dripping, screaming child to his mother. "I hope you brought dry clothes."

Beth sighed and hugged the little boy to her breast. "I did." Shaking her head, she looked at her sister. "Thanks. He has a way of getting into trouble."

"He's a boy!" Sally said as she climbed up the bank to make sure Phillip was all right. "I'll take over the fish you throw on the bank, Emily. Beth can watch the little ones."

Emily shivered as she stepped back into the cold creek. It didn't take her long to start trying to capture the salmon in her bare hands again. A little later she straightened up to rest her back. "How many do we need?"

"A lot," Sally answered. "We'll salt some and smoke some, and I for one would like fresh salmon for supper."

"Mommy, you let that one get away," Tommy complained.

"All right. We'll get back to work." His mother laughed as she picked up the fish that were still flopping at the edge of the creek.

Emily scanned the creek bed. "It doesn't look as if we took any. The water is still thick with fish!"

"Oh, but look here! How will we ever clean all these?" Beth asked, pointing to the growing pile of fish.

≈

"I thought you might need some help." Jonathan stopped to look at the scene before him.

Emily stood barefoot in the creek. Her bonnet had come off and was hanging by its strings. Her beautiful chestnut hair was loose and fell down her back in a cascade of curls. She had tucked her skirt, by now heavy with water, into her apron so her legs were bare to the knees. Her apron, also wet, had apparently been used to dip more than one fish out of the creek. When she saw him she looked down at once, as the red stole into her cheeks. Jonathan had never loved her more.

"We sure could use some help," Beth said quietly, breaking the spell. "I have no idea how to clean a fish. I've only just learned how to hit them on the head!"

Jonathan laughed. "That's the first step."

"I caught lots of fish," Tommy said as he waded out of the creek. "Now I'm hungry, Mommy."

"The working man should have some lunch," Jonathan said, patting the little boy's back.

Meanwhile Emily had fastened her hair back up and pulled down her skirt. "I packed some corn bread and leftover meat," she told Tommy, walking over to the cart.

"Phillip tried to catch a few too," Beth said as she wiped the baby's wet hair off his face. "I guess he tried to follow Tommy when I wasn't looking, but Emmy pulled him out."

She spread out the quilt they had put in the cart for the little ones to ride on. "Let's have a picnic!"

"It looks as if I arrived in time to eat." Jonathan laughed as he picked up Abbie and set her on a corner of the quilt.

"I'm going to sit on that log in the sun and see if I can get my feet warm," Emily said, taking a piece of bread and moving away from the group.

"May I join you?" Jonathan asked, sitting down a little distance from Emily. He could sense her embarrassment at being caught in such disarray.

She avoided his gaze. "That would be fine."

"Emily, you are beautiful. I don't expect you to dress like a lady when you're working on the frontier, though," he whispered. "I'm proud of you. There is no task you won't set yourself to conquer. You work as hard as most men to make our lives better." He reached out then to take her hand. "You're my best friend."

She lifted her eyes to his. "And I look forward to spending the rest of my life with my best friend."

He could scarcely hear what she said, but her words filled his heart to overflowing.

Just then Tommy shouted, "Let's go catch more fish!"

The mood was broken, but the words were embedded in both their hearts.

Emily smiled, hiking up her skirt and wading back into the water. "God has been generous with the salmon," she declared, looking at the never-ending stream of fish swimming up the creek.

Jonathan dug a pit in the sand and started cleaning fish. He threw the guts into the hole he had dug and piled up the fish for Sally to wash. "Here's a sack to put them in when you're finished." Jonathan paused long enough to toss the cloth bag to Sally.

With full tummies Abbie and Phillip settled down on the quilt to nap, and Beth returned to hitting fish on the head.

"I can't feel my feet anymore," Emily moaned. "Tommy, aren't you cold?"

He grinned and tossed another fish on the bank. "It's not too bad. Papa's going to be proud of all the fish I got."

"Yes, he is," she agreed.

Sally stood up. "We should think about going home. We have a lot to do in order to finish caring for this salmon."

"And you want to see if your husband might be there," Beth said with a twinkle in her eyes.

"That thought had come to mind," Sally admitted, smiling warmly.

"Put the children in the cart, and I'll carry the sack of fish," Jonathan told them.

"Will they all fit?" Emily asked, noticing the fish Sally was still washing.

"We could use our aprons to carry more," Beth suggested.

Emily pulled on her stockings. "Mine couldn't be any more fishy."

The happy and successful fishermen headed back to the cabin.

"Papa!" Tommy yelled when he saw the wagon. "I caught the most fish!" He threw himself into the man's outstretched arms.

"The salmon must be running," Father said, reaching over to take Abbie from the cart before giving his waiting wife a kiss on the cheek.

Sally held out her hands. "I smell like fish!"

"We all do!" Beth said.

"I need to get into dry clothes. Tommy, do you have something dry to wear?" Emily asked.

"Yes," Sally answered for him. She squeezed her husband's hand before going into the cabin to get the bundle she had brought that morning.

"How was your trip, Pa?" David asked, returning from the field. "I saw the wagon come up the path."

"I did fine. I got the nine cents a barrel for the ashes and found everything on the girls' list." He turned toward the sack Jonathan laid on the ground. "Now it looks like we have salmon to fillet and smoke."

"Will you cook one, Papa?" Tommy asked, hanging on to his stepfather.

"The way you eat, I'd better cook more than that." He hugged the boy. "Now I need to put you children down and help David get a fire going."

"I'll get wood!" Tommy started for the woodpile.

"Not until you get into something dry," his mother called.

"Mind your ma," Jonathan told him. "I'll get Pa some wood."

&

"Are you warm now?" Beth asked her sister. Emily had just changed into a dress and was carrying her wet skirt outside to dry.

"Yes." Emily feared her sister would censure her about her behavior at the creek.

"You did a good job of fishing, little sister. And it looked as if you had fun doing it," she added with a smile.

"Jonathan saw my legs bare," she said in shame.

"Emily, you aren't in Mother's drawing room. You're on the frontier. I don't think you're a fallen woman!" her sister said sharply. "Now hang up that skirt and come help me cook supper for all these people."

seventeen

Darkness had fallen before the men had unloaded the wagon. As they sat down to enjoy supper, Mr. Miller said to his wife, "I think we should stay the night." He smiled at Jonathan. "And we won't make you move outside. We can share your loft."

"I'll fix a mattress for the children next to mine," Emily offered. "I'm glad you'll stay. We need Sally to show us how to salt the salmon."

"How many did you bring in?" Mr. Miller asked.

"We could use more," Jonathan told his father. "We should salt as much fish as we plan to salt pork."

"I'll catch more," Tommy said eagerly.

"Why don't we men spear some tomorrow? We can fillet what the women caught and prepare it for salting. While they salt it, we can fill up a few more sacks," the older man suggested.

"Pa, you take David and Tommy and go. I've picked out an oak tree I want to cut down and drag in. I need to rough out some boards for making furniture," Jonathan said.

Emily gazed into his blue eyes and saw his love there. Knowing he wanted to furnish his cabin for her, she wished the time would pass and a letter would come soon from her father.

The women cleared the table and washed the dishes, while David and Jonathan sat by the fire and listened to their father tell what he had seen and heard at Fort Ontario.

"The ships will go back and forth until the lake freezes. I hope we can keep the trade with Canada going. It makes a good way for us to be able to sell our goods and buy what we need."

"Why wouldn't we keep trading with them?" Emily asked, refilling their coffee cups.

Mr. Miller smiled. "They're still a colony of England. The English are not too happy with us for winning the Revolution."

"Will there be trouble?" Jonathan asked.

His father nodded. "There could be. I even heard talk of smugglers using the harbor near here if the borders close."

Beth looked worried. "I don't like the sounds of that. Do you think it will happen?"

"Not for awhile. We'll go on as we have until we have to change."

Morning came early. The men kept busy preparing the fish for salting, while the women fixed breakfast. "The nights are getting cold. We almost had a frost last night," Jonathan said, as he picked up a fish. "Winter will be early this year."

"I heard geese going south as I came by the lake on my way back. We should take a day or two to hunt," his father suggested.

"Right now we need enough fish to fill the smoker again."

"Will you bring that barrel out of the root cellar for us?" Emily asked Jonathan.

"Do you need a sack of salt too?"

"I can use the ones from the cabin. But I can't haul a barrel up the ladder of the cellar."

He tossed the fish fillet into the waiting bucket, brushing her arm. Her heart seemed to skip a beat.

"I'll wash up and get the barrel for you," he said softly.

Sally poured the salt and showed the sisters how to layer the fish. "Do you know how to freshen it before you cook it?"

"Yes, I used to cook salt codfish a lot at home. My father liked it made in milk gravy and poured over potatoes," Emily said.

"It should be good with salmon too. Anything is better than just plain boiled fish."

"Emily did all the cooking at home. She must start teaching me before she moves to her own place," Beth told Sally.

Emily straightened up from the barrel. "That could be a

long time." She sighed.

"Don't give up, Emmy. It will happen," her sister encouraged.

With the fish salted down, the women decided to bake. They filled the oven with wood to burn down while they mixed batter and boiled beans ready to bake.

"It sure smells good in here," Jonathan said, coming in a few hours later. He took the cup of tea Emily offered him.

"Did you cut the tree down?"

He nodded over the cup. "I came to get one of the oxen to pull it back here. I've cut off the limbs and will pull those to the pile to chop up for firewood." He set the cup down. "But first would you take a walk with me? We need to harvest our apples."

Emily looked at her sister, who smiled and nodded slightly. "Go. Sally and I will take care of the oven."

She pulled her shawl around her shoulders and followed Jonathan's broad frame out the door. His sandy blond hair gleamed in the sunlight. She had forgotten her sunbonnet and patted her own hair to make sure the ends were not loose.

"I didn't think there were apples," she told Jonathan, trying to keep up with his long stride.

"They don't usually bear fruit for four or five years, but I found a tree growing here when we arrived. Let's see how many apples it has."

They walked through the rows of saplings to a spot in the woods. "Hold out your apron," he instructed her, dropping one ripe red apple into it.

"Oh, it looks so good!"

"It isn't very big. But next year there will be more, and they'll be bigger." He picked another apple and placed it in her apron.

He climbed up to reach the top of the tree and dropped the last apple into her apron.

"Are there enough apples for a pie?" he asked her as he climbed back down. "David told me before we came out here that you made the best apple pie in Connecticut."

"I don't have any lard for crust," she said, basking in his praise.

"You will when we butcher the hogs next month. The apples will keep till then."

"Then you'll have your pie," she promised.

"The best in Connecticut?" He smiled and reached out to help her carry the apples, brushing her hand, then squeezing it lightly.

She looked at him shyly. "I could cook in Connecticut, but in New York I burn the biscuits," she reminded him with a smile.

"You'll be the best cook in New York too," he told her tenderly.

When they arrived at the cabin, the men and Tommy had returned with more fish.

"I've started a brine for soaking the fish to smoke," David told his brother. He looked at Emily's apron. "Apples! Congratulations, Jonathan! I didn't think they would grow here."

"They're from a tree that was here already, but I did nurture them along. We're going to store them until we have lard, then Emily has promised me a pie." Pride echoed in Jonathan's voice.

His brother clapped him on the back. "And are you going to share that pie?"

"There should be a small taste for everyone." Jonathan joined in the laughter.

"If this keeps up we'll need a cider press," Mr. Miller told his sons.

Just then they heard a sound and turned to look up at the sky as a formation of geese flew over.

"It's about time to go hunting," Mr. Miller said.

"The fish will be smoked by tomorrow. How about the day after if the weather is good?" Jonathan asked.

The father and sons planned their trip.

Emily took the apples to show her sister and Sally. "I'll put them in the cellar till I can make a pie." Returning from the cellar, she walked over to Sally. "The men are going to hunt geese. What do we do with geese?"

"It depends on how many they shoot. I've heard they're good smoked." She stopped to pull a pan of baked beans out of the oven and put it on the shelf to cool. "I think we could also roast a goose in the oven."

"I'm willing to try," Emily declared.

"Have you plucked chickens?" Sally asked.

Both women nodded. "What does that have to do with geese?"

"Well, you pluck the geese, and ducks too, if they shoot them, then you'll have feathers for a feather bed."

Emily hid her face in embarrassment.

"You'll need one," Beth told her, smiling. "We can use some of the homespun for a cover. You should cut that out and start sewing so you'll have a place to put the feathers."

Emily tried to ignore her embarrassment and nodded. "It will take a long time to stitch around a feather tick."

"Let's find out when they plan to hunt," Sally said.

"You should come back over so you can share in the roasted goose," Beth invited.

"We will. Soon enough we'll be snowbound. I heard the men at the fellowship last Sunday say we're in for a hard winter. They claim they can tell by how much fur the rabbits have grown."

"We have wood in and lots of food for both families," Emily said.

"We must thank the Lord for taking care of us," Beth admonished.

"Yes, He has. I can't help but thank Him for being so good to me," Sally said quietly.

None of the girls spoke for a few minutes. Sally broke the silence.

"I was thinking earlier—while we're snowbound we'll have lots of knitting to do. The children need heavy sweaters. Do you have your spinning wheel going yet?"

"Yes, we do. I'll start right away on the bags of wool Papa Miller brought back from Oswego," Beth said. "While Emmy sews a feather tick, I can spin yarn."

"George set up my loom, so I can weave my flax into linen."

"Let's go and see how they're doing with the fish and find out about this hunting trip," Emily said, standing up and going to the door.

The men had salted another barrel of fish for George and Sally to take home. "I need to get back to take care of my animals. Can you gather up the children and your things, Sally?" her husband asked. "Then we'll start for home."

"I milked and fed your cow this morning when I went out to cut wood," Jonathan told them. "I brought a jug of milk home."

"I appreciate having milk for Phillip," Beth told her father-in-law.

"We'll find a way to get milk to you in the winter. What we don't drink, I'll make into cheese," Sally promised.

"I'll be back in two days," Mr. Miller said as they pulled out of the yard, and Sally and the children waved good-bye.

꙳

David and Jonathan were up doing chores before daybreak. Their father arrived as the sun started over the horizon.

"Let's go!" he urged. "The geese should land in the meadow to feed at dawn."

By afternoon they were back with both geese and ducks tied to a pole David and Jonathan carried between them.

"What do we do with all those?" Emily asked.

"I want to try smoking a couple of geese. They'd be good to take to the fellowship on Sunday. I guess we need to share more than the word of the Lord," Jonathan said with a smile.

"I guess I'll have to pluck them all." Emily looked at the stack of birds and sighed.

"I'll help you," Jonathan said, coming to her side. "Will these feathers appear in my cabin like that big rug did?" he asked, grinning.

Emily felt her face flush. "I'm making a feather tick," she admitted quietly.

"And I'm cutting up that oak tree to make a bed to put it on," Jonathan told her in a soft voice.

"You two can pluck, and we'll clean the birds," David offered.

"I'll get the cover Emmy has ready for the feathers." Beth hurried to the cabin.

"You can pluck mine, then I'll head for home. It's getting dark early now," Mr. Miller said.

Emily kept her head down while she pulled feathers. She felt the dilemma of people wanting to help her but the shame of preparing a bed for a man to whom she wasn't married. *You will marry him. It isn't wrong to prepare for a wedding,* an inner voice seemed to assure her. *And if I don't marry him, then he'll have a bed for his cabin,* she told herself sadly.

"Let's put some of these ducks on a spit over the fire," Beth suggested.

Emily welcomed the chance to be busy. As soon as the last bird had been plucked, she took four of the cleaned ducks and prepared them for the spit.

"We'll go again in a few days," Mr. Miller promised, starting for home with a sack of birds over his shoulder. "We need to fill up Emily's feather tick."

Sensing her feelings, Jonathan put his arm around her. "Did you have a hope chest in Ashford?"

She nodded. "We brought some of the quilts out here."

"You're just making a place to put the quilts, Emily. It isn't wrong to be prepared."

She looked into his face. "I want this feather tick to be for us to share."

"It will be," he said, pulling her closer to him.

eighteen

"There's frost out there this morning," Jonathan announced as he entered the cabin after feeding the stock.

"The colors are beautiful. It's as though God is painting the leaves red and gold to celebrate," Emily said, handing him a mug of coffee.

"We are celebrating!" Beth said. "Phillip is a year old." Hearing his name, he started to howl. "And hungry as usual." His mother laughed.

"I have mush ready," Emily said.

"Are we going to bring in the rest of the squash and pumpkins today?" Beth asked. She carefully spooned the cornmeal mush with milk and maple sugar into her son's open mouth.

"I could use a bowl of that mush," David said, stepping into the warm cabin and joining his brother at the table.

"What's the weather? Will it rain?" Emily asked, dishing up a bowl of mush for David.

"It looks as if it's clear and cold right now."

"We need to harvest the rest of the garden then," she told her sister.

As soon as the men were fed and the dishes cleared, the sisters bundled up Phillip and headed for the fields near the cabin. Emily dragged the small cart they used for the children.

"Phillip can ride out, but we'll need to take turns carrying him back," she said. "Some of those pumpkins are really big. They'll be heavier to carry than the baby."

"He isn't much of a baby," Beth said. She set Phillip on the ground where he promptly tried to climb onto one of the biggest pumpkins.

"This is going to take several trips," Emily said, piling the squash and pumpkins in the cart.

"We'll have to put more in your root cellar. Mine is getting full."

"The bounty of the Lord," Emily said as she laid one more squash on top.

"You pull the cart, and I'll carry Phillip," Beth told her sister.

As they approached the cabin, they saw Rufus Wheeler ride into the yard. "They must have more corn to grind," Emily commented.

The women reached the cabin in time to hear David greet Rufus. "What brings you out on this bright day?"

"I have bad news. Ned Drumhill's corn crib burned to the ground," the boy announced.

"How did that happen?" Jonathan asked, stepping up beside his brother.

"It must have been a spark from an outside fire. They think the wind came up and blew sparks into the dry corn stalks."

"Is anyone hurt?" Beth asked.

"No, and he saved his barn and cabin. The animals are all right, but now he doesn't have enough feed for winter."

"When do we gather?" Jonathan asked. His brother was nodding in agreement.

"Tomorrow—I'm riding to everyone in the fellowship and asking for help," the boy told them.

"We'll be there. Do you need more bark to build another shelter?" Jonathan asked.

"No, Pa says the people living closer can bring that," Rufus said, trying to quiet his horse.

"We'll bring corn and fodder from our supply," Jonathan said.

"Good—so far everyone has offered to share."

"That's the Lord's way," David stated.

"It must be eight or ten miles to the Drumhills'," his brother said. "We'll load our wagon tonight and be on the path as soon as there is light to see by."

"And we'll send food to feed the workers," Emily told Rufus.

"You'd better send enough for a couple of days," Jonathan told her. "We'll work until dark and sleep in the wagon. We won't be able to see to come back till dawn the next day."

"Speaking of cooking, my sister Harriet wants to know if you'll copy out your recipe for Spider Corn Cake," Rufus told Emily.

"Is she going to write another song?" Emily laughed.

"No, she's trying to learn to cook. She's doing pretty good too," the boy bragged.

"I'll bring it to the next fellowship," Emily promised.

"I hope it doesn't snow by then," Beth muttered.

"If it does, we'll still have enough light to go to the fellowship a few more Sundays," Emily assured her.

"Have you been to our pa's yet, Rufus?" David asked.

"No, I'll ride that way next."

"We can let him know. He'll want to go to Ned's with us anyway."

"Good. Then I'll keep notifying the fellowship people." Rufus rode off with a wave.

"I guess we'll need to harvest pumpkins and squash another day. What will we send for the men to eat?" Emily asked her sister.

"We've got milk and eggs. Let's make a pumpkin custard," Beth suggested.

"It'll be nice when we have lard and can make pies," Emily said wistfully.

"If this weather stays cold, we'll butcher the hogs in the next couple of weeks," Jonathan said. All of a sudden he grabbed Emily around the waist and twirled her in a circle. "I want my apple pie!"

"Put me down!" she squealed. "We shouldn't be playing when our neighbors have suffered a loss," she added sternly.

"Ned is lucky it was only the corn crib. We should thank

the Lord it wasn't a lot worse," David said.

Jonathan let go of Emily. "You're right. Now let's pull that wagon over to our corn crib and start loading some corn and fodder for Ned."

The sisters each picked up an armload of wood for heating the oven and walked toward the cabin. Phillip toddled behind his mother, carrying a small branch in his hand.

"He's going to be my big helper," Beth said, guiding him through the door into the cabin.

Early the next morning, the wagon was loaded with animal feed, food for the workers, and quilts for David and Jonathan to sleep in. "We'll leave as soon as we can see the path," David told his wife.

"Pa said for us to pick him up on the way to Ned's. Sally has milk and some of her cheese to send along with the sacks of fodder Pa was getting ready," Jonathan told them.

"God has been so generous to us this year. This is our way of giving back," Emily said as the men prepared to leave.

"You're right, Emily. When we give to the Lord's people, we are giving to Him," Jonathan agreed. The look in his eyes gladdened her heart.

With the men gone, the sisters went back to gathering squash and pumpkins. "Let's pile them next to the corn crib. When the men come back with the wagon, they can take them to your root cellar," Beth suggested.

"Jonathan's root cellar," Emily said quietly. She looked at the sky that had darkened. "It feels cold enough to snow and still no word from Father. How long will it take?"

Beth put her arms around her sister. "I don't know. I pray everyday that we'll hear something. But remember—if a letter can't get through, Mother can't expect you to travel back to Ashford."

"I wish I believed that. She thinks it's easy to get to the stage at Fort Schuyler."

"Well, you won't ever have to find out if it's easy or

impossible," Beth stated firmly. "Father will get the letter from Mr. Richards and act on it."

Emily sighed. "I hope you're right." She picked another squash to add to the pile.

That evening the girls sat by the fire shelling beans. "I'll take the pods out to the pigs in the morning," Emily promised. "I hope those boxes we have for holding the lard will work."

"I remember Kate rendering lard, but I've never done it," Beth said.

"I did it the fall before we came out here. By then, Mother didn't want Kate to do anything but the washing."

"I wonder what made her get so close-fisted with money?"

Emily giggled. "Making me do Kate's work didn't help. I know Father paid her the same wages he always had."

"That's good. Kate needed the money to take care of her mother," Beth said as she added beans to the basket.

"I'm sure Father will move her into our house when her mother dies. He told me once that Kate grew up with Mother. It seems she was good to Mother when others scorned her."

"Well, I'm glad Kate is there to take care of Father."

"Yes, I am too. Mother got so she wouldn't even fix him a cup of tea." Emily continued to toss beans on the growing pile.

"Do you think we will get like that?" Beth wondered out loud.

"I hope not," Emily said firmly, as she picked up an apron full of bean pods to be shelled.

❧

The men returned late the next day in a swirl of snow.

"If this keeps up very long, we'll have to put the runners on the wagon," David said, entering the cabin.

Jonathan followed him with the empty dishes the women had sent food in. "Everyone sends thanks for your donations. Especially the pumpkin custard."

"This Sunday may be our last fellowship till spring, so I

invited people here. Is that all right?" David asked his wife.

"If you'll ride to Sally's and get more milk, I'll make more custard," Emily said.

"She sent two jugs home with us," Jonathan told her. "I have more things to bring from the wagon, but could I have a cup of hot tea or coffee first?" He shivered and clapped his hands together to warm them.

"We'll be crowded with everyone in here, but it will be wonderful to see our friends before winter." Beth sighed.

ᔥ

The next Sunday, after everyone at the fellowship had shared the Scriptures and eaten the food spread out on the table, the women and young children lingered in the cabin to visit. The men headed for the barn or stood outside smoking their pipes and talking about what crops they would plant in the spring.

Harriet Wheeler made her way over to Emily. "Did Rufus ask you for the recipe?" she asked timidly.

"Yes, I copied it out for you. Let me get it."

EMILY'S SPIDER CORN CAKE
1½ cups cornmeal
1 tablespoon sugar
1 teaspoon salt
l teaspoon baking soda
2 eggs, beaten
2 cups buttermilk
1½ tablespoons melted butter

Heat a 12" iron skillet (spider) in a hot oven.
Sift dry ingredients. Combine eggs and milk and
stir into cornmeal mixture. Stir in butter last.
Pour into hot spider, in which you have melted 2
tablespoons of butter to coat the bottom. Bake 30
minutes in a hot oven.

"I hope I can cook as well as you someday," Harriet said, taking the paper Emily held out to her.

"Rufus told us you are doing very well."

"Really?" Harriet asked in surprise.

Just then Emily noticed Harriet's mother standing nearby, talking with others in the group. Both the girls turned to hear what she was saying.

"Pastor Barnes has headed for Rotterdam," Mrs. Wheeler told the women. "He said he'll start his circuit here in the spring." She smiled. "I know he's trying to get his son-in-law to settle here and be our full-time preacher."

"He's not only a preacher, but a tanner and a shoemaker too," someone added.

"We could certainly use his crafts," someone else said.

Emily didn't hear any more that was said. Her heart felt like lead with the news that Pastor Barnes would not be back until spring.

That's months away. How will I make it through the winter?

Standing with the others to pray, she added her own silent prayer that her father would receive Jonathan's letter and respond.

The fellowship ended with many prayers for a safe and healthful winter. People started leaving amid sad farewells. It would be long months before they could meet together again. Bible study would be a family arrangement during the snow-bound days of winter.

"With the weather staying cold, let's butcher those hogs," Mr. Miller told his sons as he and Sally prepared to leave.

"Come over the next clear day, and we'll take care of it," David said.

ঌ

"I don't want any part of this," Beth declared when her father-in-law arrived for the butchering.

"It's a mess, I know," Emily agreed.

"You girls stay in the cabin. We'll let you know when we

have the meat ready to salt down."

"I'll get the brine ready for ham and bacon," Emily said.

It took most of the week for the hard-working crew to prepare the pork for winter.

"I'm glad we could render the lard outside," Beth said. "It smells terrible."

Emily laughed at her sister. "It does smell, but it tastes so good to have shortening to cook with."

"Jonathan took a load of squash and some of the pickle crocks out of our cellar and put them into his. Now we'll have room for the barrels of salt pork. David says we can hang the ham and bacon in the corn crib when they're out of the smoker," Beth said.

Tired from all the work of preserving the pork, Emily fell into a sound sleep that night. Pepper slept nearby. When he stirred, she rolled over, thinking the dog was dreaming. Then she heard his soft growl.

She rose to a sitting position. The sound she heard sent a shiver down her spine. "I had hoped never to hear that again," she whispered, putting her arm around the dog when he crept close to her.

Jonathan hurried down the ladder and grabbed his gun. David burst out of his corner pulling on his pants. "What is it?"

"Wolves. The hog butchering must have lured them in," Jonathan said. He took his powder horn and headed out the door.

"We'd better get them before they get our chickens." David grabbed his gun and followed his brother.

The men rushed out of the cabin, leaving Emily trembling in terror.

nineteen

"Phillip is asleep," Beth whispered as she pulled her shawl around her and sat on the mattress next to Emily. "What is happening?"

"Wolves. They must have smelled the blood from the hog butchering." Emily kept her arms around the dog.

Pepper stayed close to Emily as if seeking protection. His deep growl still rumbled whenever they heard the wolves howl.

Beth shivered. "They sound scary. You told me you saw them when we were on the way out here."

"I never want to see them again," she said, as visions of the gleaming teeth and menacing yellow eyes appeared sharply in her memory.

"It sounds as if they're getting closer. What will they do to the men?"

"The men took guns. I think they'll be all right," Emily said, without conviction. Another howl rent the air, sending the women and the dog closer together. As they huddled in fear, they heard a gunshot.

"I hope that scares them away," Beth muttered.

Another shot rang out. Then silence filled the room. Leaning close with the dog in front of them, the sisters waited.

"I'm too scared even to pray," Emily admitted.

"Me too. Thank God Phillip is not awake. He would sense my fear."

They heard something being dragged outside the cabin. "Do you think the wolves got one of the men? Would they drag them away?" Beth clutched her shawl tighter around her shoulders. Her face was white with apprehension.

"I don't think so. I think they eat their prey right where they kill it. Do you want me to look outside?"

"Are you brave enough to do that?" Beth asked in wonder. "My knees are shaking so much that I don't think I could stand up."

Just then the door burst open, and Pepper jumped up and barked. Jonathan entered the cabin with David close behind.

"We got two of them. The rest ran off," Jonathan said proudly, his face flushed with excitement.

"What do we do with wolves?" Emily hoped she wasn't in for another week of preserving meat. *I don't think I could eat anything that looks so evil. But I guess I can if Jonathan wants me to.*

"We buried the pigskins and offal, and still the wolves came in. That's how we got them. David and I laid in wait by the buried pigskins and shot them when the wolves tried to dig them up. We think we'll use Pa's skiff and dump the wolf carcasses in the lake."

"After we skin them," David reminded his brother.

"Why do we want wolf skins?" Beth asked, still clutching her shawl.

"They're worth ten dollars," Jonathan said. "If we get enough of them, we can pay off our land." He poured water into a basin to wash up.

"Who would pay for the skins of such horrid animals?" Emily asked with disgust.

"There's a ten-dollar bounty on wolves. We'll salt down these hides until we can get them into Whiteside and collect our reward," Jonathan said eagerly. "I may try to hunt some more of them."

Emily shivered. "I never want to see or hear another wolf as long as I live."

Jonathan walked over and put his arm around her shoulders. "I'll keep you safe."

Emily sighed. She felt safe in his arms, but she still didn't want to hear or see another wolf. Silently, she prayed Jonathan would not hunt them again.

Mr. Miller arrived the next day. "Did I hear wolves around here last night?"

Beth nodded and took down a mug to pour her father-in-law a cup of coffee.

"Jonathan and David are out back skinning two of them," Emily told him.

"Two! That's wonderful!" he exclaimed, accepting the cup from Beth. "I'll just take this coffee with me and check on them."

Emily looked at Beth and shrugged as the older man left. "Sometimes they're almost like little boys. I'm going to pray every night that God will feed the wolves so they don't come around here. I don't want Jonathan out hunting those evil creatures." She shuddered at the thought of the wolves.

"I have yet to see one, and I hope it stays that way if they scare you that much," Beth declared, sitting down at her spinning wheel.

"I'll put the jugs of milk he brought where they'll stay cold. Then I want to try to sew some more on Jonathan's shirt. Maybe I can think about something good instead of those horrid animals."

"Are you going to give the shirt to Jonathan for Christmas?" Beth spun yarn onto a spool.

"I haven't decided, but seeing the snow does make me think of Christmas. I hope we can go to Sally's for Christmas dinner." Emily sighed and took the homespun shirt out of her pile of sewing. "Spring seems a long way off."

"But if it keeps snowing, you can't go home. Count your blessings."

"It also keeps a letter from Father from reaching us." Emily threaded her needle and started to stitch the collar on the shirt. "But we have to wait for Pastor Barnes to come back in the spring anyway." She sighed again. "I wonder if I will ever get married."

"You aren't an old maid—yet," Beth teased.

The women worked until the men came in looking for a meal. "The skins are taken care of. Pa says we shouldn't take the carcasses to the lake. We'll haul them back into the woods and leave them for the varmints."

"Does that include wolves?" Emily asked, her voice trembling.

"If it does, we'll shoot a couple more for the bounty," Jonathan declared.

Emily shivered but said no more.

❧

Snow continued to fall. "We don't get snow until December in Ashford. Why is it so early here?" Beth complained to David.

David shrugged. "Pa says it didn't snow until almost Christmas last year. Mr. Wheeler and some of the others who have lived here awhile said we were in for a long, hard winter. We have food, wood, and shelter and will have to make the best of it."

Beth sighed and went back to spinning yarn, while Emily sat on a bench knitting socks.

"Can we still get through to Sally's?" Emily asked her brother-in-law.

"Can you use snowshoes?" He laughed.

"I will if I have to." She clicked her needles rapidly.

"Why would you have to? Did Beth kick you out?"

"No." She giggled. "But I might go mad if I have to sit here and knit socks for the next six months."

Beth laughed. "You could always switch to knitting mittens."

David looked bewildered. "You haven't been in the cabin a month, and already you're acting up. Mr. Wheeler was right. It will be a long winter with you two." He bent down and kissed his wife.

"When is Jonathan coming back?" Emily asked David.

"He's working at his cabin and should be back by dark."

It was past dark before they heard Jonathan in the yard. Emily looked out their window and saw him head for the barn to check on his horse. *I hope someday to get as much attention as that animal,* she grumbled to herself.

When Jonathan came in the door, he set two jugs of milk on the table. "I came home by way of Pa's. Sally sent some milk and a block of cheese." He pulled a package out of the inside of his coat and put it next to the milk.

"Was the snow deep going over there?" David asked.

"Yes, and it's snowing again." Jonathan poured himself a cup of tea from the pot on the hearth. "Abbie is real sick. Sally is worried about her, so Pa said he wouldn't be over for awhile."

Emily put her knitting down. "Does she need help? What's wrong with Abbie?"

Jonathan sat on a bench across from her. "Her chest is congested. She has a fever and can't breathe well." He sipped the hot tea. "I don't know what anyone could do for her." He shook his head and set the cup back on the table.

"Could you get me over there, Jonathan?"

He looked at Emily with interest. "Why? What can you do?"

"I don't know if I can do anything except encourage Sally. Sometimes another woman can comfort a friend," she added softly.

Jonathan sighed and picked up his cup. "I guess I could break a trail with snowshoes, and you could follow me."

Emily looked at her sister. "What do you think?"

"I think one of us should go, and I can't leave Phillip."

"I'll get a bundle together. Can we leave in the morning?"

"The snow is drifted too deep for the sled, but if you're willing to walk, I'll help you." Jonathan's look said he would keep her safe if he had to carry her.

As soon as it was light, Emily set off behind Jonathan. The snow had stopped, but the wind blew the new fallen flakes in whirls of white around them.

"Can you see the way?" Emily asked through the scarf she had tied around her face.

"I know the way even when I can't see the blazes," he assured her. "I can follow the opening in the trees where the path is."

It seemed to take hours to make any progress. By the time they saw the smoke from the Millers' cabin, Emily was ready to drop with exhaustion. As soon as she walked through the door, Sally threw her arms around Emily, snowy cloak and all.

"I am so glad to see you! Come over by the fire and get warm while I pour you a cup of tea."

"How is Abbie?" Emily saw the mattress on the floor by the fire and knelt by the pale child. Smoothing the little girl's hair off her forehead, she glanced up at Sally. "She feels hot. Has she had the fever long?"

"Three days now. Her chest hurts so much that she cries until she can't breath. I don't know what to do."

"I don't know much about sick children, but I thought I could take care of the chores and leave you free to take care of Abbie."

"Having you here will be a big help," Sally said with warmth as she handed Emily a cup of hot tea.

Jonathan had gone out to the barn to see his father. When he came in, he took off his coat and hung it on a peg. "As soon as I warm up, I'll start back. We don't have many hours of daylight this time of year." He sat down at the table and took the cup Sally offered him. "Pa says he'll see that you get home, Emily."

She looked up at him. His gaze, first at her, then at the sick child, sent a quiver down her spine. *He's thinking we'll have children.* Brushing Abbie's fevered brow she thought, *I hope none of them ever gets this sick.*

"I'll stay as long as I can be of help," Emily said, going over to join Jonathan on the bench.

He took her hand and squeezed it. "I hope you'll be home soon." Then he took his coat down from the peg before kneeling next to the sick child. "Get well soon, Abbie," he whispered.

Emily took over the cooking. Neither Sally nor her husband ate much. Tommy enjoyed being with Emily and devoured the food she put in front of him. Sally sponged Abbie's face with a cold cloth, trying to break the fever.

Mr. Miller and Tommy had gone to the barn to care for the animals when Emily heard a knock at the door. She watched Sally hurry to answer it.

Colonel Dewey walked into the cabin and looked from one woman to the other. "My wife send this." He held out a small leather pouch to Sally. "You make tea for sick child. This will make better."

Sally took the pouch and motioned to the Indian. "Come, sit by the fire and get warm."

"I'll pour you a cup of tea," Emily said, taking down a cup.

Colonel Dewey squatted in front of the fireplace. Looking at Emily he ordered, "You make tea for child."

Emily nodded and traded the cup in her hand for the pouch Sally was holding. Sally poured tea and gave it to the Indian, while Emily opened the pouch and studied the dried herbs. With a silent prayer, she emptied them into a cup and filled it with hot water.

"I will let it cool a bit," she told Colonel Dewey. She knelt down next to the child on the same level as the Indian. "How did your wife know Abbie was sick?"

"God spoke to my woman," he said. "She knows the ways of medicine." He pointed to the cup Emily held. "Will make child better. Now I go."

He rose and started for the door. "Thank you," Sally said. "George is in the barn. Will you tell him what you have brought us?" she asked politely.

The colonel nodded and left.

Emily held a spoon to the child's lips and slowly fed her some of the medicinal tea.

"Do you think God spoke to Colonel Dewey's wife?" Sally asked in awe.

"We have been praying. I believe the Lord spoke to the Indian woman. She collects herbs, and He told her the ones that will cure little Abbie," Emily said quietly.

twenty

Within hours of drinking the herbal tea, Abbie's fever broke, and she slept soundly. The congestion in her chest eased so she could breathe without pain.

Emily sat by the little girl so Sally could get some much-needed sleep. "I'll call you if there's any change."

Abbie woke in the morning looking bright and refreshed. "Can I have some mush?" she asked.

Sally turned toward Emily to hide the tears from her daughter. "I feared she would slip from me just as her father did," the distraught mother whispered. "Thank God for sending Colonel Dewey." She busied herself making a pan of mush to serve her family.

Abbie remained weak but sat up and listened to the Bible stories Emily told her. She retold the stories so the little girl could understand them. Tommy sat beside his sister and listened to the age-old stories too.

"Tell the one about David," Abbie begged Emily.

"I don't know what we would have done without you," Sally said, handing Emily a cup of tea later.

"I haven't done anything," Emily sipped the hot tea.

"You've been here for us. You've prayed for us, and the children love you. You need a houseful of your own." Sally smiled at her.

Emily sighed as she leaned against the table. "I don't know what the future will bring. I can only trust God."

"When there's a break in the weather, I'll take you home," Mr. Miller told her. "The snow keeps piling up. I fear the sap will be late to start running this year."

"I'll be glad when it does run. That will mean spring is coming," Emily said.

"And a letter from your father," Sally said quietly.

Emily smiled. "We have Christmas coming before spring. I'll think about that instead of wishing my life away." She set her cup down. "Will you be able to get to our place for Christmas?" she asked Mr. Miller. "We have the big oven and can bake more things than Sally can with the reflector oven."

He looked at the sleeping Abbie. "With our little girl healing, we'll make every effort to be together as a family."

&

The sun shone brightly when Mr. Miller and Emily started out. The older man carried a pack with milk, butter, and cheese for his son's family.

"Sally makes the best cheese I've ever tasted," Emily told him.

"I hope someday to have more cows. We could even set up a small creamery to make cheese to sell." He plodded ahead of Emily with his snowshoes to pack the snow where she could walk.

"It would be popular. When she brought some to the fellowship last fall, everyone liked it." Emily placed her feet in Mr. Miller's steps.

The walk back did not seem so far. *I feel like a horse headed for the barn,* Emily thought. *I'll be close to Jonathan by nightfall.* She shifted the bundle she carried.

Mr. Miller did not tarry long with his sons. "I want to be home by dark." He smiled at Emily. "And I want to see my little girl who is getting better."

Emily sat down across the table from Beth. "Tell me everything," Beth pleaded.

Emily repeated the story of Colonel Dewey and the herbs.

"You really think he was sent by God?" Beth asked.

"Yes," she said quietly. "We prayed, and the Lord sent the cure." She looked up and smiled. "He does work in mysterious ways."

"I pray He'll make it possible for Papa Miller, Sally, and

their children to be here for Christmas."

"I asked them here because we have the big oven."

"You're right—we can bake more things. It will be a treat for everyone in the middle of this awful winter."

"I've been thinking about gifts for the children." Emily joined in the spirit of planning.

"You have the shirt finished for Jonathan," Beth reminded her.

"Yes, and now I want to make a doll for Abbie." She looked over her teacup at her sister. "Remember you teased me when I picked all that fluff off the milk weed last fall?"

Beth looked puzzled. "Yes."

"I plan to use it to stuff a rag doll and make a stuffed animal for Phillip."

Setting the cups aside, the women brought out their bundle of material. "I can use this homespun to make the body of the doll." Emily picked up some scraps left from Sally's wedding dress. "Do you think there's enough here to make a doll dress?"

"Let's get started!" Beth said, her face glowing with excitement. "We still have to knit and mend, but we'll find time to make fun things."

One evening Emily was stuffing the body, legs, and arms for the doll. "What will we make for Tommy?" she asked suddenly. "I almost forgot him!"

"A barn for his animals," Jonathan suggested. He was sitting by the fire with a cup of coffee. "I have some wood scraps at my cabin where I've been making furniture. I'll bring some here, and we can make him a place to keep all the animals Pa carves him."

Emily looked at him, not even trying to mask the love she felt. "That's a wonderful idea."

"What are you making Phillip?"

"A bear," she said, laughing. "I'll make him a stuffed bear he can chew on, instead of that big black bear who wanted to chew on Phillip." Emily pointed to the bearskin stretched across the far wall.

The next night Jonathan came in with a bag of wood scraps. Sitting next to him in the firelight, Emily felt content. He carved and formed the wood into a small building, while she stitched the body of a small bear.

"I think I'll make a fence to go around it. That way Tommy can see the animals instead of hiding them inside the barn." He held up what he had put together.

"He'll be pleased." *I wonder if we'll sit together making gifts for our own children someday.*

All things in God's time, she reminded herself.

With the evenings spent on making things, the time went quickly. Beth made a small quilt to go with the doll. Emily made a dress and sunbonnet and braided hair of yarn.

"Abbie will treasure this as much as we did our fancy dolls with the china heads," Emily declared, holding the finished product up for her sister to see.

"It's the things made with love that mean the most," Beth agreed. "I love the shoe-button eyes," she said, pointing at the shiny black eyes on the doll.

"I want to put them on Phillip's bear too. Do you think he'll chew them off and swallow them?"

Beth thought for a moment, her brows furrowed. "Put them on. We'll tell him to chew only the ears so the bear can't hear, but the animal has to see where it's going."

Emily laughed. "You think he'll understand that?"

Beth shrugged. "He eats dirt and rocks and still thrives. He'll survive a shoe button."

"We need to start thinking about Christmas dinner."

Beth shivered. "As cold as it's been, it will be nice to have the oven heated up. Do we have enough wheat flour for pie crust?"

"I saved some. We can make pumpkin pies. Do you think we could have fresh meat?" Emily groaned. "I get tired of salt pork and salt fish."

"Why can't the men bring in venison? They tell us how bad this winter is for the deer to find feed. One less will make more food for the others," Beth reasoned.

Emily giggled. "I like the way you think. I'll ask Jonathan to go hunting. He says he sees deer all the time on his way between here and his cabin."

"And I'll send David with eggs for Sally and have him bring back milk and butter."

"Now we need to pray the weather will be good so we can all be together," Emily said as she put down the bear body she had been stuffing.

&

The weather did stay clear for a week. Mr. Miller and his sons walked the path between their cabins enough times to pack the snow down. On Christmas Day, he was able to hitch an ox to the small sled and bring his family to David and Beth's home.

Emily and Beth had baked pies and bread. They cooked potatoes, squash, and carrots. The night before, they had heated the oven and left a big venison roast to cook all night.

"Oh, it smells good in here," Sally said, hugging both young women at once.

"I hope you brought some cheese," Emily said as she hugged Sally in return.

"Yes, and more milk and butter. The vegetables taste so good with butter." She sighed. "I will never forget dry johnny-cake and boiled fish and forever thank God for good food."

"Amen," they all said together.

"Look at you," Emily said as she picked Abbie up. "You have bright rosy cheeks. Are you all better?"

The child nodded her head. "The tea made me better."

"She's getting her strength back. I think she has gained some weight," Sally said, smoothing back the copper-colored curls on her daughter's head.

"We have enough food cooked to put weight on all of us," Emily declared.

The family settled down around the table to exchange news. The men talked of when the sap might run.

"You think it will be late this year?" Jonathan asked.

His father shrugged. "It's been a hard winter. I don't know how that will affect the trees. When I see Colonel Dewey again, I'll ask him."

"Well, if I'm going east, I'd better leave right away. I want to be back in time to help with the syrup."

Emily stopped what she was doing. East? Did he say he was going east?

"Jonathan!" she cried. "You can't go in this weather! You'll get lost! The snow is higher than the blazes on the trail."

He looked at her with an expression that melted her heart. "I can't wait, Emily. I'm needed here. If I'm to go to your father, it must be now."

Emily's emotions churned. *I want my father's blessing, but what if I lose Jonathan getting it?* She fought back visions of Jonathan buried in a snow bank. Unwanted, the wolves howled in her mind. *Oh, what should I do?*

"Jonathan, I would rather live as we are than to have you die trying to get east this winter."

"I can't live like this, Emily. I want you as my wife. I want our children. I will go east in the next few days."

Emily could not look at the people around her. She stared at her folded hands. *If he dies, they will never forgive me. Please, God, help me do what is Your will. Keep Jonathan safe.*

Beth stood up from the table. "We'll talk of this later. Now we need Pa to read to us."

"You're right," Mr. Miller agreed, reaching for the Bible. "Bring the children close so they can hear," he instructed his wife. He opened the book to the words written in Luke. The Christmas story poured over the little family in the wilderness.

Emily felt the love from that stable of long ago and trusted

God to guide her. *He gave His son for us. He will show us the way.*

"Tommy, we have a surprise for you," Jonathan told the boy when his father closed the Bible.

Tommy looked wary.

"He probably thinks the surprise is the dress we made his mother." Emily laughed.

Jonathan brought the barn and fence and put it on the table. "Do you have some animals with you?"

With his eyes glowing and a smile that filled his face, Tommy pulled carved animals out of his pockets and started filling his barn and barnyard.

Emily looked at Abbie sitting on her mother's lap. "Do you have a doll?"

Abbie took her thumb out of her mouth and shook her head.

Beth came up behind the child and put the doll and small quilt on the table.

Abbie looked first at her mother for approval then hugged the doll to her chest. "I call her Emmy?" she asked.

Emily felt the tears well up in her eyes. Before they fell, her sister gave Phillip his bear. He pounced on it and promptly started to chew an ear.

"I knew he would like the ears!" his mother said.

Everyone laughed.

Other gifts came out of hiding. Jonathan stroked the shirt as if it were fine silk.

"I will wear it with pride," he told Emily. "I couldn't bring your present here. You know we have furniture in our cabin." He smiled lovingly. "I also made you a chest to put your quilts in. They didn't look right lying on the floor in the corner," he said with a grin.

Emily closed her eyes. *I can't let him risk his life for me. I will go against the commandments before I let him die.* She opened her eyes to tell him she would marry without her father's blessing, but before she spoke she heard a knock at the door.

David opened the door and greeted one of Colonel Dewey's sons. "Come in and join us," he said, holding the door open wide.

"I have message," the Indian told the group. "There are supplies waiting for you at the Four Corners. Snow is too deep for driver to come here."

"That's good news. Now come and join us for dinner. It's Christmas, and we welcome the stranger at the door."

twenty-one

The Indian entered the cabin cautiously. Emily thought he looked exhausted.

"Did you come straight here from the Four Corners?" David asked, urging the young man to sit at the table.

He nodded.

"We need to get food on the table," Emily whispered to Beth and Sally. The women opened the oven and pulled out the roast. Emily could see the Indian looking hungrily at the meat.

As soon as the women had pans of food on the table, Mr. Miller spoke. "Let us return thanks for the bounty God has given us." He asked a brief blessing and took up a knife to carve the venison. He put a large piece on a plate in front of their guest.

The Indian looked bewildered.

"Eat, Friend. You must be cold and hungry after that long hike," Jonathan urged.

Their friend did eat. He piled up the offered vegetables and took more meat. When Emily put a piece of pumpkin pie in front of him he looked at her with a puzzled expression.

"Try it," she suggested.

He took a bite, and a smile flickered across his stoic face. "You teach my woman to make this?"

Emily smiled. "Yes. Will your woman teach me about plants and herbs?"

She was rewarded with a smile and a nod of his head before their guest devoured the pie and handed his plate back for more.

Everyone ate heartily of the food the women had prepared. With coffee mugs full, the men sat back, while the women cleared the table.

"Can you tell us what is at the Four Corners?" Jonathan asked the Indian.

"Much barrels and big sacks. You will need a sled to carry," the man replied.

Jonathan and David exchanged worried looks. Their father sat next to the Indian. He knew a few words of the man's language and asked about the conditions to get to the Four Corners.

When Emily came to fill the coffee cups, she heard Mr. Miller tell his sons, "He says the snow is deep. We won't see the blazes unless we dig down to them." The older man sighed. "I don't know if we can get the oxen through the drifts or not."

"If you'll drive the oxen, David and I can snowshoe a path before you. We could shovel the biggest drifts out of the way," Jonathan suggested eagerly.

"Let me talk to Colonel Dewey," his father said. "He can give us directions and an idea how to get the sled there and back."

"I go," the Indian said, standing. He walked to the women and gave each of them a nod resembling a bow.

"I would like to meet your woman. She can teach me much," Emily said.

His face remained stoic, but she could see a light in his eyes.

Emily tried to hear what the men were saying. *There must be a letter from Father. It will be dangerous for them to travel in this snow. But five or six miles are a lot better than Jonathan trying to go back to Ashford alone,* she reasoned.

Beth remained silent. Emily put her arm around her sister. "They won't go if it isn't safe. Your father-in-law wouldn't put his sons in danger." She turned to Sally. "Will you stay with us?"

Sally shook her head. "I'll have to take care of the animals. We'll stay tonight. The cow was milked this morning, and we'll get back early tomorrow."

Christmas ended with a feeling of excitement. What

awaited them at the Four Corners?

Mr. Miller took his family home the next morning. It was dark when he found his way back to his son's cabin the next day. "I left before dawn to find Colonel Dewey," he told his sons. Sitting on a bench, he took the cup his daughter-in-law offered him. "I think we can do it." He explained how they would travel, and they made plans to start out in two days, if the weather allowed.

❧

Jonathan tried not to show his excitement. *Even if Mr. Goodman's blessing is there, we'll have to wait till the preacher comes in the spring.* He peered out at the drifts of snow reaching to the roof of the cabin. *When will spring come?* He glanced at Emily and knew her thoughts were an echo of his. Walking over to where she sat knitting, he took her hands in his.

"You will be my wife in a few short months," he said softly.

He could see her sigh. She looked up at him with so much love his heart contracted.

"We have waited almost a year," Jonathan whispered.

"A year in which we have become friends forever," she answered.

Two days later, the men left before light. David and Jonathan walked on snowshoes ahead of the oxen. The beasts had been in the barn for weeks and seemed to welcome the fresh air.

The first hour went well. Others had tramped through this part of the woods, and the men could easily see the path. As the day wore on, they clambered into unbroken snow. "Let's see if we can find the blaze on the trees so we know we're heading in the right direction," David suggested.

"Here," Jonathan called. "The snow isn't as deep here, and I can see the mark. Let me go ahead and find the line of blazes."

Their father urged the oxen to follow. "We should reach a meadow before we get to the Four Corners. But we need to follow the sun to know the directions there."

Jonathan glanced up at the gray sky. "Maybe it will clear," he murmured to himself.

They struggled on. Jonathan's legs felt like logs. Stomping through drifts of snow to pack it for the oxen left him dragging one snowshoe in front of the other. He looked at his brother who appeared about to drop.

"Should we rest?" he called to David.

"We'd better keep going," his brother yelled back. "The daylight won't last. It'll be dark by late afternoon."

"How are you holding up, Pa?" Jonathan shouted to his father.

"We're doing fine. The oxen are in good shape and will pull as long as we need them."

Thank God it wasn't a winter like this last year. David and Beth and the baby would never have made it to New York. And neither would have Emily. Jonathan plodded on with thoughts of what life with Emily at his side would be like. *Keep us safe, Lord. Take us back to the women and children who wait for us.*

They caught a glimpse of the sun when they reached the meadow Colonel Dewey had told them about and were able to set their course northeast. By dusk they saw the lights of the Four Corners ahead.

"We don't get visitors this time of year," the innkeeper told them. "Come in, though. You are more than welcome."

"Where can we put our oxen and sled?" Jonathan asked.

"There's a barn out back. Help yourself."

David and Jonathan unhitched the oxen. After they fed and watered them they joined their father.

The innkeeper had hot coffee waiting for them. "I have a pot of stew cooking. We'll eat shortly."

"Do you have letters for the Millers?" Jonathan asked, taking a cup from the man.

"I was so excited about having guests that I forgot," the innkeeper apologized. "You didn't travel in this snow to spend time with me." He reached up on a shelf and handed

Jonathan three packets. "You also have a lot of goods stored in my back room. The driver who brought them couldn't get any farther."

Jonathan tore open his letter. "Thank God!"

"You heard from Edward Goodman?" his father asked.

Jonathan nodded his head. "He sends more than his blessings. He apologizes that he didn't get my first letters." Jonathan waved the letter. "And he has sent us a wagonload of gifts."

David held up his letter. "I heard from Mr. Richards. He offers me part interest in his mercantile. It seems Henry has run off with some of his father's money."

"Will you do it?" Jonathan asked.

"No," he said, picking up his coffee mug. "Beth and I will make our home here. I still plan to have my own mercantile someday. But Mr. Richards will help me get started."

"What happened to Henry?" Father asked.

David looked puzzled. "His father says only that he ran off and took the money out of the safe. He said he was sorry for any grief his son had caused us. I don't know what he means."

"Well, he's the one Mrs. Goodman wanted Emily to marry. Maybe that's what he means," Jonathan suggested. "None of it matters now. I have permission to marry Emily." His energy was renewed by the joy.

"Do you have a preacher in your settlement?" the innkeeper asked.

"No, the circuit preacher is in Rotterdam for the winter but promised to come to our place first in the spring," Jonathan told him.

The innkeeper laughed. "Well, for your sake I hope spring is early this year."

The Millers were up early and loaded their sled in the dark. "We can see the marks in the snow from yesterday. Let's start out now," Jonathan suggested.

His father laughed. "Could we eat some breakfast first? Getting home is not going to bring spring any sooner."

The pain of the day before had disappeared. Jonathan felt

as if he could float over the snow.

"We could make it home within daylight," David said brightly.

"We can't push the oxen too hard," Father reminded them. "They have a heavy load to pull. I hope we don't sink into the snow we came over yesterday."

Dawn seemed to take a long time to break. The sky remained dark in spite of the faint light in the east. Jonathan's euphoria began to ebb as he watched the storm build. "Once we're in the trees again, we may be more protected," he yelled to his brother as the wind whipped around them.

The snow began to fall. The wind blew it in swirls, blinding them. Jonathan glanced back often at his father in the sled. Sometimes the snow blocked him out of sight. *Stay with us, Lord. Keep us safe,* he prayed. He slowed his pace so he could keep his father in sight.

They entered the trees, but the snow and wind continued to whirl in a white sheet around them.

"I can't see yesterday's path!" David cried.

"Stop a minute, Pa! Let me look for the blazes on the trees!" Jonathan yelled back toward the sled.

"It's getting worse," David said when Jonathan came back. "Can you see anything?"

Jonathan nodded his head. "Yes, I can see the ruts from yesterday, and I spotted a couple of blazes. But if this keeps up, I don't know how much longer yesterday's path will show."

Father had stepped down from the sled to brush the snow off the oxen. "We'll keep going as long as we can, but maybe we should watch for a place where we can find shelter."

They moved on at an even slower pace. "Check the blazes again!" Father shouted. "We don't want to go in circles."

Jonathan tried to find his way. *It all looks alike. I don't even know which trees to dig down to.*

"It isn't good, Pa. I can't find the trail or the blazes."

"Let's find a place where we can settle in. Get the oxen on the lea side of the sled. We can find room inside under the canvas for protection." He shook his head. "There's no reason to keep going when we don't know the way."

David and Jonathan unhitched the oxen and tied them to the side of the sled.

"If they wander off, we might never find them," Jonathan worried.

"I'll get what hay is left in the sled and put it underneath where they can eat it before it blows away."

"Can we get a fire going? We could melt some snow and make coffee."

"We could take a little of this hay for tinder," David said as he pulled the feed out of the back of the sled.

"Maybe we could melt some snow for the animals to drink." Jonathan dropped the sticks he had gathered next to the straw and pulled out a flint.

"They'll eat the snow," his father told him. "Can we move some of those barrels around inside so we have room to sit down?"

"I'll help you," David said, while Jonathan tried to make them something hot to drink.

The men huddled together. "Emily sent corn bread," Jonathan said, pulling out a bundle. "There's some jerky in here too."

"We'd better ration it out. We don't know how long we'll be stranded here," his father said quietly.

"Are we lost?" David asked.

"We'll know when we can see again."

"As soon as the blizzard lets up, I'll try to find the blazed trail again," Jonathan promised.

The wind and snow continued throughout the night.

Dear Lord, did you bring us this far only to let us wander in the woods? Jonathan prayed. *Was I too selfish? Did I risk my brother and my father just so I could find out if Mr. Goodman would let me marry his daughter? Please, Lord, protect us. Help us find our way home.*

twenty-two

"Stop it, Emily!"

Emily froze in her steps. *She sounds like Mother!* she thought in horror.

"You didn't force the men to make this crazy trip. They knew the risks and went anyway."

Emily sat down again by the fire and quietly picked up her knitting. "It has been dark for hours. They won't be home tonight."

Beth stood by the fire stirring the pot that hung there. "Do you want something to eat?" Her tone had softened.

"No, thank you. I'm not hungry." The knitting needles continued to click.

"I'm going to have a bowl of stew, then go to bed," Beth told her.

Emily continued to knit and pray. When the candle on the table sputtered out, she put her work down and pulled her mattress out of the corner. Pepper lay down beside her.

Both women were up before daybreak. Emily put some corn bread on the table, while Beth poured coffee.

"The storm has stopped. When I went out to feed the chickens and Jonathan's horse, it looked as if it might stay clear today," Emily said.

"They should be home by dark." Beth picked up her coffee mug and a piece of bread. "Why don't you get out some of the dried berries and make a pie? It will be a treat for the men when they get here."

Tension filled the air. *If something happens to David, I will have to go back to Ashford with Beth, and she will always blame me,* Emily thought as she rolled out the pie dough.

Later that afternoon, Emily went out to collect eggs and check on the chickens and the horse. She heard them before she saw the sled.

"They're coming!" she shouted to Beth. Pulling her shawl around her, she ran through the snow toward the sound.

David drove the oxen. Jonathan jumped down from the sled and ran to sweep Emily into his arms. Then he bent down and kissed her lips tenderly. In that moment, time stood still for her.

He stepped back from her. "You'll catch your death of cold out here, Emily. Go back to the cabin while I help David with the oxen. I'll come inside shortly."

Reluctantly she obeyed. Her sister stood in the door with Phillip in her arms, and Pepper trotted out to greet the men.

David pulled the wagon close to the door and jumped down to hug his wife and son, while Jonathan started unhitching the oxen.

"They've worked hard and deserve a good meal." Jonathan led an ox to the barn.

"Where's your father?" Beth asked David.

"We took him home on the way, and Sally sent milk and butter," David said, leading the other ox away.

Coming into the warm cabin to the good smells of fresh baked pie, both men hugged their women before sitting down at the table.

"Tell us what happened," Emily insisted, still clinging to Jonathan.

"Maybe they need food first," Beth suggested.

"Sally fed us bean soup and corn bread," David said.

Jonathan pulled the letters out of his coat. "I have a letter from your father."

The glow on his face told Emily the news was good.

"I think you'll want to read what he has written you first." He handed her a packet.

"Beth, come read over my shoulder. This is to both of us."

My dear daughters,

    I am filled with joy. I thought you were lost, and now you have come back to me. When I did not hear from you I feared the worst. Grief filled my days.

    When Mr. Richards brought Jonathan's letter to me, I cried with joy. I thanked God that you were safe and still cared for me. I cried that you had suffered by my lack of knowledge.

    I cannot make up for the past, but I have sent gifts. They are but a small token of all that I would like to give you. I am sorry I will not be there to see my baby girl married, but I know she has found a good man who will care for her.

    I ask you to find it in your hearts to forgive your mother. I can't believe she meant to harm you. Please, in mercy, pray for her.

Emily could read no farther. She turned into Beth's arms, and the two women wept together.

Jonathan and David looked at one another. "Let's unload the sled," Jonathan said, and they left the weeping sisters.

A few minutes later, when Emily and Beth saw the barrels and sacks, they became as excited as little children.

"What's in this?" Emily asked, poking a sack.

"There were four sacks of wheat flour. We left one with Sally and Pa," Jonathan told them, dropping a large bundle on the floor.

Beth cut away the heavy burlap, exposing a bolt of light pink cloth with dark pink flowers. She looked up at her sister. "Your wedding dress!"

"Did Father send that too?" Emily asked.

"No, Mr. Richards did. His letter is not clear, but he seems to be apologizing to us for Henry."

Emily laughed. "There is no apology for that ugly man.

But why would his father think he's to blame?"

David shook his head. "I have no idea." Then he turned to his wife. "Where do you want this barrel?"

"Leave it here where we can open it. I won't know where to put it until we know what it contains."

"I'll take the top off for you," Jonathan said.

Emily looked at the straw inside. Pulling some aside, she held up a china teacup. "Look, Beth! These are Mother's prize cups. Why would she send them to us?"

Beth giggled, took the cup, and held it up with her little finger extended and her hand on her hip. "I can't imagine, but shall we invite Sally for tea?"

Emily laughed as she continued to pull straw and dishes out of the barrel. "There's some paper in here," she said, digging deeper and pulling out what appeared to be a letter.

"It's from Kate. Her spelling is terrible. Let me read it to you."

> *Der Mis Emly an Mis Lizbeth,*
>   *I aint much fer writin but you shuld no all thats ben goin on. Yur pa movd me in when my ma died. Hes ben unhapy sens you gurls lef. He dont spen much time at home wit yur ma. Mr. Richars giv hm a lettr n the fall. I nevr sen yur pa so mad. He crashd in the hous like a mad bull. Yur ma took to er bed. He yelld at er which he nevr don befor. When he charjd thruh the parlr he tipd ovr er sewin basqet and found all the lettrs you sen but he nevr saw. I feard he wuld have appoplecksy. A few days aftr that Hnry Richars ran off wit a tavrn gurl. I herd he stol mony frum his pa. He usd ta com ta see yur ma an we no now he tuk the lettrs frum the mur- canteel and brot them ta her. Yur ma has takn ta ladunum and dont leeve her room. I takes care*

ov her. Yur pa tol me ta pak the dishus fer you an
anethin else I thot you wud like. You rite me an
tel me if ther r mor things I can sen.
  Yur luvin frend, Kate Smithers

⁂

"Well, now we know why Mr. Richards apologized," David said, hugging his wife to his side. "He even offered to take me as partner in the mercantile."

Beth stood up straight, an anxious look on her face. "Will you do that?"

"No, our home is here. I'll ask him to help me get a mercantile started here as the town grows."

"First tea parties and now we're building a town?" Jonathan laughed. He started gathering up the straw Emily had spilled on the floor. "I just want to grow apples."

Emily glanced at him shyly. "And raise children."

⁂

The excitement continued as the four adults worked through each day. They had to bring in wood and keep the fires going, prepare the food, and care for the animals. The sisters stopped knitting so they could cut and sew Emily's wedding dress.

"I can't believe I am finally going to be married," Emily said, stitching tucks in the bodice of her dress.

"You've had a year to find out if you like frontier life."

"And become better friends with Jonathan," Emily admitted. She looked up from her sewing. "Do you really like it here? Would you like to go back and have David go into the mercantile?"

Thoughtfully Beth put her needle down. "I do like it here. It will be lonely when you move to your own place, and I'll have a lot more of the work to do. But I want to stay. I could never live as our mother has, thinking only of herself, attending fancy social gatherings, and being waited on by servants."

"With Jonathan and me gone, you won't have as many people to cook for, and you won't be as crowded either."

"But we'll have to grow just as much food and preserve it for winter," Beth replied.

"Sally is always here to teach us what to do and help us." Emily started sewing again.

"Hasn't she been a blessing? Can you imagine having to figure all this out by ourselves?" Beth smiled and took up her needle too.

Jonathan entered the cabin, bringing the cold air with him. "I've been over to Pa's and brought you some milk and cheese." He put the jugs and package on the table. "He's been talking to Colonel Dewey. It seems the snow acts like a blanket to keep the ground warm. He says the sap will run soon, and it'll be a good year for syrup."

"With all this snow, how will you get to the sugar camp? How will you tap the trees? One day you'll tap them, then the snow will melt, and you'll need a ladder to get to the buckets," Emily fussed.

"You're a bundle of good news," Jonathan said, smiling as he bent to kiss her cheek. "The snow will start to melt before we can get into the sugar bush. And, yes, I want spring to arrive as much as you do, but we'll have to take it as it comes."

"Did you start the apple seeds Father sent?"

"You're starting to sound like a wife." He swept her into a hug. "Yes, they're in dirt at our cabin. I keep a fire going there most of the time so they won't freeze. We'll expand our orchard again this spring." He kissed her forehead. "You'll become the best apple-pie baker in New York."

They enjoyed two weeks of good weather in February, and the snow started to disappear. "We cleared the path to the sugar camp," David announced when he and his brother came in for supper one evening. "I think we'll be tapping trees in another week."

Emily's spirits lifted. "Spring can't be far away," she whispered to Jonathan as she leaned over to fill his coffee cup.

"I've got more shelves built so you can take your china

cups home," he told her, holding her hand when she offered him a plate of bread.

"Home," she sighed. "Maybe Beth and I can pull Phillip in the cart with the dishes and put them away."

"We should do it tomorrow. There's no telling how long this good weather will hold," Beth said.

The snow fell again, and David and Jonathan had to clear the path to the sugar bush again.

"We were tapping trees the middle of February last year. Let's try a few trees to see if the sap is running," Jonathan suggested.

The sap flowed, so the three men worked and lived in the sugar bush. Emily took the Indian cart full of food to them as often as she could get through. She and Jonathan spent every moment they could making plans for their life together.

"Did you bring pie?" Jonathan asked, hugging her when she pulled the cart to a halt at the camp.

"Are you only going to marry me for my pies?" she asked in fun.

"You caught me! But you're the best baker in New York." He bent to kiss her, making her forget the cold walk to camp.

"Tell Beth I'll be back in a couple of days. We need more jugs to put syrup in, and I'll need to bring the sled to get them. Do you want some fresh syrup to take back?" David asked.

"Sure! And I didn't burn the biscuits in your food bundle. You can have syrup with those."

"That sounds good. Have you been to see Sally?" Mr. Miller asked.

"I went there yesterday and brought you cheese, butter, and milk from her. Tommy wanted to come back with me, but Sally told him I had to ask you first because you're so busy now."

"I miss that little boy. Tell him I'll bring him out to camp before the sap stops running." He grinned. "You'd better tell my wife I miss her too."

The men had learned how to make the syrup, sugar, and molasses. They shaped their camp into an efficient production line as the boxes of sugar and jugs of syrup piled up in the root cellar.

"We'll have a lot to trade at Fort Ontario this year," Jonathan told the sisters when he came in with more to store away.

"Our cellar is so full that you'll have to start storing some at your place," Beth told him.

"We could move some of the vegetables over there too," Emily said, thinking of the meals she would cook for Jonathan.

"You're right, Emily. You'll be moving there soon."

The snow didn't disappear quickly. The drifts against the back of the cabin shrank, pouring water into the swelling creek.

"Will the boxes wash away?" Beth asked her husband. "The creek is over its banks."

"I'll check on them when I go over to our place," Jonathan told her. "Do you want me to bring back potatoes? I still have a full bin in our cellar."

Warmth spread over Emily. *It will happen. I will marry Jonathan.*

The snow melted, and mud came. Paths that had been blocked by snow were now impassable through mud. Each day Emily would look out and pray the sun would shine and dry up all the standing water and muck.

"Don't wish your life away," her sister said, coming to the door to put an arm around Emily.

The trees started to bud. All the apple trees had come through the winter. Even the small seedlings Jonathan had put in the year before poked up from the dirt with swelling leaves.

When the trilliums started to bloom in the forest, Pastor Barnes arrived at the door.

Jonathan greeted him warmly. "I have the letter from Emily's father. How soon can you marry us?" he asked, bringing the man into the cabin.

"I'll ride to the fellowship tomorrow," David said, and Emily squeezed Jonathan's hand in delight.

Beth urged the men to sit down and have coffee while making plans, and Emily brought out some fresh bread and butter.

"Will we be married here?" she asked her sister.

"Where else?" Beth asked in surprise. "We're family. We'll send Jonathan out to get venison, and we'll serve a big roast to the wedding guests."

"And the guests will bring johnnycake." Emily laughed.

&

Sunday dawned bright. It was as if God smiled on the wedding party gathered at the Millers'. The women shooed the men out of the cabin. They crowded around Emily as she put on her new pink dress. Harriet Wheeler had woven a crown of wild flowers for Emily's hair.

"You're a beautiful bride," Beth whispered.

Trembling with excitement, Emily walked to Jonathan's side. He held out his hand to her, and the look on his face showed he felt the same joy as she did. The two stood by the apple orchard that had blossomed for the occasion. While making their vows before God and their friends, Emily thought of her father and how much she wished he could be with them. But as she gazed up at her new husband, her sadness disappeared in the love she saw in his eyes. He held her in his arms and kissed her lips, and she thought no more of anything but the life they would share.

A Letter To Our Readers

Dear Reader:

In order that we might better contribute to your reading enjoyment, we would appreciate your taking a few minutes to respond to the following questions. We welcome your comments and read each form and letter we receive. When completed, please return to the following:

Rebecca Germany, Fiction Editor
Heartsong Presents
PO Box 719
Uhrichsville, Ohio 44683

1. Did you enjoy reading *Sweet Spring* by Marilou H. Flinkman?
   ❏ Very much! I would like to see more books
      by this author!
   ❏ Moderately. I would have enjoyed it more if

   _____

   _____

   _____

2. Are you a member of **Heartsong Presents**? Yes ❏ No ❏
   If no, where did you purchase this book?_____

   _____

3. How would you rate, on a scale from 1 (poor) to 5 (superior), the cover design?_____

4. On a scale from 1 (poor) to 10 (superior), please rate the following elements.

   _____ Heroine   _____ Plot

   _____ Hero   _____ Inspirational theme

   _____ Setting   _____ Secondary characters

5. These characters were special because_____

_____

_____

6. How has this book inspired your life?_____

_____

_____

7. What settings would you like to see covered in future **Heartsong Presents** books?_____

_____

_____

8. What are some inspirational themes you would like to see treated in future books?_____

_____

_____

9. Would you be interested in reading other **Heartsong Presents** titles?   Yes ❑   No ❑

10. Please check your age range:
    ❑ Under 18   ❑ 18-24   ❑ 25-34
    ❑ 35-45   ❑ 46-55   ❑ Over 55

Name _____

Occupation _____

Address _____

City _____ State _____ Zip _____

Email _____

····Heart♥ng····

HISTORICAL ROMANCE IS CHEAPER BY THE DOZEN!

Any 12 *Heartsong Presents* titles for only $27.00 *

Buy any assortment of twelve *Heartsong Presents* titles and save 25% off of the already discounted price of $2.95 each!

*plus $2.00 shipping and handling per order and sales tax where applicable.

HEARTSONG PRESENTS TITLES AVAILABLE NOW:

(If ordering from this page, please remember to include it with the order form.)

Hearts♥ng Presents
Love Stories
Are Rated G!

That's for godly, gratifying, and of course, great! If you love a thrilling love story but don't appreciate the sordidness of some popular paperback romances, **Heartsong Presents** is for you. In fact, **Heartsong Presents** is the *only inspirational romance book club* featuring love stories where Christian faith is the primary ingredient in a marriage relationship.

Sign up today to receive your first set of four never-before-published Christian romances. Send no money now; you will receive a bill with the first shipment. You may cancel at any time without obligation, and if you aren't completely satisfied with any selection, you may return the books for an immediate refund!

Imagine. . .four new romances every four weeks—two historical, two contemporary—with men and women like you who long to meet the one God has chosen as the love of their lives. . .all for the low price of $9.97 postpaid.

To join, simply complete the coupon below and mail to the address provided. **Heartsong Presents** romances are rated G for another reason: They'll arrive *Godspeed!*